Mirrored

by

J L Wilson

A Remembered Classics Romance, Book 9

Mirrored

Cover Art by *Kim Mendoza*

The Wild Rose Press, Inc.
PO Box 708
Adams Basin, NY 14410-0708
Visit us at www.thewildrosepress.com

Publishing History
First Edition, 2022
Trade Paperback ISBN 978-1-5092-3933-7
Digital ISBN 978-1-5092-3934-4

Published in the United States of America

"She was strangled and put in the car. She was murdered before they even left their house."

Somehow, I wasn't shocked. All the little odd things from the last few days started to make sense. Finn, acting so odd. Vaughan insisting on me finding "Mr. Right Now." Royal, defending Finn's odd behavior. Even the coincidence of all the women in our group dying.

All the women except me.

"Snow?" Royal's voice was gentle, almost kind. "Are you—"

"You don't get to call me that." I kept my voice as steady as I could. "I'm Natalie DeWitt to you."

Royal flinched as if I'd hit him. "I never lied to you."

"But you never told me the truth."

His lips twisted in a half-smile. "Shades of gray. Coming from a woman who only wears black, white, and gray."

I went to the window and stared at the yard outside. I could only make out the silhouette of trees. Clouds covered the moon, and the darkness was complete. "And red. Don't forget the red." The word reminded me of the glass in my hand. I took three gulps of wine and set the glass on the end table. I was afraid if I held it any longer I might throw it at him.

Dedication

For all the caregivers and all that they do

Chapter 1

"You signed me up for what?" I jerked off my goggles and dropped them on the workbench, grabbing a rag to wipe my sweaty face. It was November outside my shop but inside it was eighty degrees and toasty thanks to the overhead heater and my welding torch.

"I didn't sign you up. I created a profile for you. All we need to do is review it and submit it." Vaughn Kern, one of my oldest and (sometimes) dearest friends, regarded me with those puppy-dog brown eyes that earned him the nickname of Hopeful in college. "You deserve to be happy."

I pushed my thick white hair back from my face, corralling it into its ponytail. "Just because I'm single that doesn't mean I'm unhappy."

"You know what I mean." He gestured around my spacious workshop, a one-stall detached garage where my tools and equipment were scattered on various work surfaces. "Wouldn't you like to share this with someone? Spend your Sunday afternoon with a special somebody, watching football, instead of doing that?" He eyed my latest sculpture doubtfully. "Whatever it is," he muttered.

"Show me a man who appreciates found objects and loud country music and I'll consider it." I drained my water canteen and leaned against the bench, shifting my stiff shoulders in my Garth Brooks T-shirt and bib overalls. "I'm not dating material. Four failed love affairs convinced me that the single life is for me."

"You were young and foolish. You're older and wiser now, ready for a mature man. Come on. Just review it." He thrust a tablet at me. "You have a lot of free time on your hands now that you're retired."

"I'm not retired. I'm just between jobs thanks to the godless bitch who married my father and made my life the living hell it is today."

Vaughn tsked. "Natalie Jean Dewitt. Such language."

I snatched the tablet from his hands and glared at the screen, using that to avoid his sympathy. I'd been pressured into selling my flower/gift shop two months earlier when my father sold his half of the land on which the business sat. My damned stepmother Aurora Raines, whom I detested with the heat of ten thousand suns, was behind it. This was all part of her ploy to make my life miserable. The bad part was that she was succeeding.

I examined the online form for a Sexy Seniors dating service. "Who uses this site? A bunch of stalkers could be set up there and you'd never know."

"It's all totally safe. Your information is protected. Besides, people need to answer so many questions, a stalker wouldn't bother. It has a triple-A rating from the Better Business Bureau. It's completely legit."

I focused on the tablet, my hopes for a quick escape vanishing. "You can't use this picture. And what's this? I know nothing about gourmet cooking." I skimmed the next section. "Nobody would believe someone could love classical music and country music."

"I thought it best to widen the net, so to speak," Vaughn admitted. "After all, you don't mind classical music."

"I wouldn't willingly listen to it, though. I can't boil water and you know it, Vaughn. If it weren't for your cooking, I'd eat out every night." Vaughn owned a catering company and kept me regularly supplied with leftovers. I studied the information. "For cryin' out loud, you make it sound like I'm a social butterfly."

"Okay, so I exaggerated a bit." He peeked over my shoulder, which was a bit hard to do because he was only a few inches taller than my five-foot-five. "What's wrong with the picture?"

"It's an old picture."

"It's only three years old."

I knew damn well how old it was. It was taken at my father's wedding to my stepmother, may she rot in Hell. "I don't look like that most of the time." I frowned at the lacy gown, the upswept hairdo, and the me-in-makeup. "Aren't you afraid of scaring away the guys with my white hair?"

"You've always had white hair. It's very pretty."

True on all counts. My thick, long hair turned white when I was in my teens, one of the reasons for my nickname. Now that I was fifty-five, I finally appeared my age. "Guys don't like women with white hair."

"How do you know? I spent a lot of time on this profile." He eyed me reproachfully, an expression of his that I knew well. That's the problem with being friends with someone for almost forty years. "Just check some of the answers I gave you."

"Answers? To what?"

He pointed to a section of the online form. "What's your idea of a perfect evening?"

"Drinking beer, cranking up the tunes, and sorting through a junk pile or digging around in a car engine," I muttered, peering at the tiny print. "Oh, cut me a break, you didn't say that." *I adore quiet nights at home with a special someone, watching a movie and drinking a fine Chardonnay.* "I hate Chardonnay, and you know it."

"Okay, we'll change it to Pinot."

I thrust the tablet back at him. "What's the rush? Why now?"

"The reunion. It would be nice if you had someone with you."

"The reunion is in a week, Vaughn. I doubt if I'll find Mr. Right in a week."

"Well, how about Mr. Right Now?" he snapped. "We're not searching for perfection here, just someone to show up on your arm, so to speak. You know that Sporty and Nimble will be there in all their married-bliss glory. Wouldn't you like to twist their noses just a bit?"

Oh, that was tempting. Thirty-some years ago, I was the ringleader of a band of Iowans who all ended up as scholarship athletes at a small northern Minnesota college. We went through four years and a couple of harrowing events together and stayed friends. Two were dead, two lived not far from me, and the remaining three were coming back for a visit a week from now, a ritual we continued every five years since graduation.

Those three had lives far away from Forestville, Iowa, population one-hundred-thousand. One was a retired pro baseball player (Nimble), now a TV announcer who married his college sweetheart (Sporty).

They often regaled us with tales of their beautiful home in Florida, gorgeous children and now grandchildren, and blissful lifestyle. Another (Nerdy) made his home in Silicon Valley and was wealthy from his investments in the Tech World.

They lived the kind of lives I only read about in magazines. I suspected a lot of it was exaggeration, but it was still annoying. I, on the other hand, could only regale people with tales of crafting sculpture from objects found in my forays into salvage yards with an occasional outing to Minnesota to visit friends and shop at the Mall of America. I loved my life, but compared to theirs, mine was Tame with a capital T.

"You won't find someone in a week." I checked my small torch to make sure it was safely shut off, then I lined up the objects I would use in the next layer of my sculpture.

"I'll bet I do," Vaughan said. "Let's see what happens. Just because someone answers that doesn't mean you're committed." He plunked the tablet on my workbench. "See—there's some good-looking guys here. I'll bet one of them is a match." He began scrolling through the list of Eligible Bachelors.

I peeked at the faces while they swept past. "Ooh, that one's interesting," I said, my interest piqued despite my best intentions. "That one, too. He might be okay."

"What about this one?" Vaughn brought up the profile of a guy with thick hair as white as mine and a stern, almost grim face and a passing resemblance to an actor whose name I couldn't remember. "He likes country music and sculpture."

"And handguns." I pointed to the Hobby section

and *skeet shooting*. "I don't do handguns."

"Handguns can occasionally be useful." Vaughan studied the profile of the guy, frowning at something he read.

"You're only saying that because you're married to a cop." Vaughan's husband, Finn Sterling, was a sheriff's deputy for Forest County. Finn, nicknamed "Calm," was the last member of our troupe of Iowa expats at the Minnesota college of my youth.

"I love the way that sounds." Vaughan grinned at me, the glow from his marriage ceremony of the previous year still evident. "Married to a cop. For so long we were just friends or partners. It's so sweet to be able to call him my husband."

I put my arm through his, grabbing my sweatshirt jacket when we walked out of my shop. I was happy for his happiness and a bit envious, too. Maybe that's why I caved in. "Okay, go ahead and find me Mr. Right Now." I pulled on the fleece against a biting November wind mixed with sloppy snowflakes.

Vaughan swept me into a hug, lifting me off my feet in his enthusiasm. "You won't regret it, you'll see."

"Just don't pair me with some foodie snob who's allergic to cats and doesn't know how to line dance. I should probably review that profile before you send it in." I walked him to his car, an enormous gray SUV with *Kern's Classic Cuisine* on a magnetic sign on the door. "Thanks for the leftovers. I'll eat high on the hog for a few days."

"I'm catering a Kiwanis luncheon and the Ladies' Auxiliary this week as well as, you know—The Thing. Now listen. We need a code word for when you're out with Mr. Right."

"What?"

"You know. A Safe Word. If you run into trouble with him, say…" Vaughan looked off into the distance. "Tarragon."

"Tarragon? What's that?"

"It's an herb. Just say it, and I'll know you need help."

"Yeah, sure. Whatever."

He waggled a finger at me. "Better to be safe than sorry. I'll drop by Wednesday night with leftovers and Mr. Right." He waggled the tablet at me then dropped it on the passenger seat. "You just wait, Snow. We'll find you your Prince Charming yet."

I stepped away from the car while Vaughan backed out of my garage drive and into the long, winding lane that served as the entry to my property. I had long ago given up on finding my prince, but if it made Vaughan happy, let him look. I doubted he'd find Prince Charming in the vicinity of Forestville, Iowa.

I went into the house, entering through the attached one-car garage into the kitchen/dining area. My home was a ranch-style with three bedrooms and a bathroom upstairs and a large family room and exercise space downstairs, with a walk-out patio to the wooded back yard. All the houses in this neighborhood were on two-acre lots but, unlike my neighbors, I had very little lawn to maintain. The trees and rolling terrain gave me a great deal of privacy, even now when the leaves were off the trees. My house sat up on a small hill, and I glimpsed Doc Small's house across Apple Lane, a quarter-mile north of the end of my drive. The other houses around me were either on a hill or hidden by trees.

I busied myself with making a Bloody Mary then dropped onto my couch, disturbing Miss Copper, my calico cat, who was dozing on an afghan next to Mr. Gold, my yellow tabby. I arranged my feet around them and leaned back to take stock of my life.

Despite what I told Vaughan, I was for all intents and purposes retired. The tiny curio shop/flower store I had owned was now sold to a retail developer who planned to put up office buildings and restaurants on that space and the land my father once owned. I was two million dollars richer and, thanks to a long-ago inheritance from the maternal side of my family, I was comfortably settled for the foreseeable future with a paid-off house and no debts. As much as I hated to sell the rambling little cottage that was my shop full of this-and-that, I knew the march of progress made it inevitable.

What pissed me off about it all was the timing. I'm sure the Evil Queen, a.k.a., my stepmother, had pushed my father into the sale now so I had to liquidate before Christmas, my favorite holiday of the year. I sold almost all the inventory and some of the store furnishings. All that remained were the floral coolers, which truth be told, were so old they would only be good for parts. I left those behind with the building when I vacated a few weeks ago.

If only they had waited until the first of the year so I could have had one last Christmas party, Christmas festival, Christmas showcase, in the store. But no, the bulldozers were already rampaging on the land a bare three weeks since I vacated. I glared at the woods behind my house and silently cursed She Who Must Not Be Named. Her marriage to my father three years earlier was a major turning point in my life—and his.

I disentangled myself from paws and went to my den at the back of the house. My desk was one I made myself from large slabs of particle board faux-painted to look like marble. Several of my paintings were hung on the wall along with photographs, mostly of me and my father. My mother died when I was a child, and he raised me through childhood and my teen years. We were business partners, too, with him running the nursery and landscaping side of our gardening business while I handled the gift shop and curio side.

All of that was changed now. He and Aurora still had one business location on the eastern edge of town, but our presence was erased here on the west side of town. I studied a picture of me and Roy, my father, at the grand opening of the west side store, Prince's Pride Landscaping, a play on words because I was his little princess. That was thirty years earlier when he was forty-five and I was twenty-five. We both had thick silver-white hair and dark, almost black eyes. Roy was almost a foot taller than me, and he had his hands on my shoulders while he stood behind me, both of us laughing into the camera.

That easy camaraderie was gone now. Aurora saw to that. She was forty years younger than him with silky blonde hair, a voluptuous body, and her eye on my father's wealth. My father was deliriously happy with his trophy wife who had, thank God, so far produced no children. That would have been the final straw.

Yes, my life took a turn three years earlier when Roy remarried, and it was turning again now. But in what direction? For the past thirty years I spent ten and twelve-hour days at the store. Now—what? Painting, photography, sculpting—I loved my hobbies, but could I spend entire days in pursuit of the perfect photograph?

I decided to postpone thinking about it and checked my email. Confirmations were there from all the college crew. *Hooray for a Snow White weekend!* Nerdy wrote, his email peppered with emoticons. *I'm not sure I can handle the temperatures, though.*

"Wimp," I muttered. "Thirty years in California has watered down your blood." Sporty said something similar in her reply. *I can't believe I'm leaving Florida to spend Veteran's Day weekend in Iowa! I must be crazy to trade temps in the 70s for temps in the 30s!* "Well, nobody could come in the summertime, so this is what we get," I said to my mail queue, filing her reply with the others. I made a mental note to get the planning underway earlier next year so the hothouse flowers would have no reason to complain.

I pushed away from the computer and went to the picture of me and my friends in college—Snow White and the Seven Jocks. We all played spring sports and were all from this part of east-central Iowa. Nimble, Sporty, Hopeful, Nerdy, Brainy, Bitchy, and Calm. Now only five, though. Bitchy—Charlene Brownlow— a girl on the golf squad with me, had died five years earlier right before our reunion, killed in a car accident when her vehicle was run off the road by another car that was never found. Then last year Brainy died, victim of a random rape and mugging. I shuddered. Two of the four women in our group, dead.

I touched the Me Who Was back then, a slender girl with long white hair and an infectious grin that said, *Bring it on, I can deal with it.* What happened to that optimistic girl?

She ended up here, fifty-five years old and not quite sure where her life was going. I shut off the light and left the past behind me. Time to figure out the future.

****

I was busy on Monday and most of Tuesday with final details surrounding the money from the sale that I was investing, and the sale of some items from my store that I had stashed in my workshop. On Tuesday evening I braced myself for what I knew would be the unpleasant highlight of my week. I pulled on black jeans, a gray and black striped sweater, and my black boots and headed for the Forest Club and my father's seventy-sixth birthday party.

They had reserved the big party room at the back of the private club for his bash. Roy and Aurora were at the far end of the room near a table laden with food and some gifts. A few of Roy's old friends were there, but mostly it was Aurora's crowd of society do-gooders and social climbers. I made my way through the crowd, pausing to greet the few people I knew.

My father appeared happy and spry with his white hair cut short, his late summer tan still evident, and his body lean and trim from years of working in the landscaping business. There was a telltale slump to his shoulders, though, and his dark eyes weren't quite as sharp as they used to be. The years were pressing in on him, even more noticeable because of Aurora, who radiated youth and vitality in her mini-skirt, high heels, and body-clinging blouse.

I spied Vaughan near the banquet table, supervising the placement of a tray of sandwiches. He glimpsed me at the same moment and made his way through the throng to intercept me a few yards from my father. "He's here." Vaughan jerked his head so hard I thought I heard a muscle pop.

"Who's here?"

"Mr. Right Now."

"What? You found someone?"

Vaughan put his hand on his chest in mock dismay. "You wound me. Of course, I found someone. I told you I would."

"You invited him to my father's birthday party? Why did you do that?"

"I figured it was best to meet him in a public place. If he could handle your family, he could handle anything. I have to admit, he's even more impressive in person."

I turned slowly, scanning the crowd. "Which one is he? Wait a minute." I shook Vaughan's arm. "You were going to let me review that profile before you submitted it. What did you say about me?"

"You look just like your picture," a bemused male voice said behind me. "I have to admit, I was worried. So many people fake their appearance on dating websites."

I glared at Vaughan. "We're not finished," I hissed at him before releasing his arm. I plastered a smile on my face and turned—and took a step back to peer up. The man facing me was at least six-and-a-half feet tall, broad-shouldered, and lanky—there was no other word for it. Slap a cowboy hat on him, and he'd be Sam whatever-his-name-was who did those voiceover commercials for trucks. The guy wore black jeans and a black shirt covered by a gray tweed jacket that contrasted with his white hair parted on the side, a long curl tumbling onto his forehead.

He held out his hand. "I'm Brendan. Brendan Royal."

I gaped at him. "Royal?"

One corner of his mouth twisted up in a self-deprecating smile. "Yeah, I know. I get that a lot."

Vaughan moved behind Royal and peeked around the man's torso. *Was I right?* he mouthed. *Mr. Right, right?* He winked at me then whirled to talk to one of the waiters going past with a tray of appetizers.

"I didn't—I mean—I wasn't sure—" I tried to find Vaughan, but he was already gone. "I wasn't sure if you'd be here," I managed to say, taking the outstretched hand.

My fingers were lost in his warm and strong grip. He didn't wear any rings, and his hands were rough but not calloused. "I wouldn't miss it for the world. It's not often I get a chance to meet such an interesting person." His hand slowly released mine, drawing back with a caress as though his fingers were exploring my bones. "You look like your father." He glanced to his left where my father and Aurora stood just a few feet away.

As though sensing his interest, Aurora turned, her icy blue gaze sweeping over me to rest on Royal. Her red-painted lips curved in a speculative smile. I could almost see the flashing light over her poufed and teased hair: *interesting older man alert.*

"Oh, crap," I muttered. "We're in for it now."

Royal leaned over me. "Excuse me?"

"My father's wife. You're just the type of man she likes."

He straightened slightly but still stayed close. Now that he was nearer, I could see he was only superficially like Sam what's-his-name. Royal's face was long and narrow, with faint dimples near his mouth and dark eyebrows over very bright green eyes. Eyes that now were staring into mine with amusement. "Really? What type is that?"

Aurora was almost to us now, posing next to another woman for a selfie. They were both like escapees from one of those Real Housewife shows. "A sexy older man," I snapped. "She specializes in them."

"I don't know whether to be flattered or worried," he murmured. "I think I'll be both and ask you to protect me."

"Snow, I'm so glad you joined us," Aurora said, slinking her way to us, her hips twitching seductively in her skin-tight leather mini-skirt.

I eyed her outfit, which was amazingly inappropriate for a cold November night. "Interesting ensemble," I said off-handedly.

"Do you like it?" she purred, striking a pose with one leg slightly extended to show off her toned thighs and high-heeled spangly pumps. "I splurged at Bergdorf's the last time we went to Chicago to shop."

"Some poor calf gave up his life for that skirt," I muttered. "What a waste."

Aurora disregarded my criticism and turned her attention to Royal. "I don't believe we've met. I'm Aurora Raines." She held out a manicured claw.

Royal said his name then added without any hesitation, "Snow and I just wanted to drop in and see how things were going before we left for the bar." He made a show of examining his watch. "Whoops, we'd better get going, sugar. Kiss your daddy, and let's get downtown and have a beer before the band starts." He put his arm around my shoulders and gave me a squeeze.

"A band? You're going to hear a band? Which one?" Aurora blinked widely. "I didn't realize you were seeing someone," she stammered.

I was hard pressed not to blink right back at her. The feeling of a male body against my side was unusual but pleasant. "I'm just full of surprises." I slid out from under Royal's arm and went to my father, who enfolded me in his arms.

"Who's the gentleman?" he asked, his gaze going over my shoulder.

"Just a guy I know." I kissed Roy's cheek. "Happy birthday, King Daddy," I whispered, using my pet nickname for him.

"Thank you for coming, Princess." He peered into my face. "I miss spending time with you. We used to have such good times together."

For an instant I felt sorry for him. The wistful look in his dark, loving eyes reminded me of the man I used to know, the father who spent countless hours reading to me, taking me with him to job sites, and attending school plays and pageants. "I know, Daddy. I wish it were like the old days."

"Maybe it will be again." He kissed my cheek. "I have plans to change things. Come by the house tomorrow morning. Let's talk." He stared into my eyes, and I saw worry, anger, and—something I couldn't quite identify. Fear? Panic?

"What is it? Has something happened?"

"Come to the house tomorrow. She says she goes to the gym but I think—she comes back early sometimes. Promise me you'll visit tomorrow. Early?"

15

He seemed worried. I automatically said, "Sure, I'll be there. I'll stop by at eight, the way I used to do before opening." Dad and I always had a morning cup of coffee before I opened the store. We would sit and talk about clients, hashing over any problems before the rest of the staff came on-site.

Except now my store was gone. I stowed my bitterness and gave him a quick hug. "I'll come to the house. I promise."

Aurora's perfume surrounded us. I drew away when she took his arm, tugging him away from me. "You must come over more often," she said, her gaze beyond me. "And bring your friend."

"Yeah, right." I smiled at Roy then turned, only to find Royal immediately behind me. For a moment I was pressed against him. We managed an awkward two-step that got us away from Aurora and her hawk-like evaluation.

"I hope you don't mind," Royal said, his voice pitched for my ears alone. "Your friend mentioned this was awkward for you. I wanted to give you a way out."

I spied Vaughan, lurking behind a floral display. He gave me a thumbs-up then vanished behind the gladiolas. "Thanks. I appreciate it. The less time I spend with the Evil Stepmother, the better off for me."

He grinned, deep dimples appearing at the edges of his mouth. "Hard to believe she's your stepmother."

"No kidding. It continues to stun me every time I think about it." I led the way out of the room, nodding to a few acquaintances on the way. We paused at the coat check for me to get my black winter coat then headed outside.

"Which way?" Royal looked around the parking

lot.

"To what?"

"Your car. You'll want to follow me to the bar, right?"

"You weren't kidding? You want to go hear a band tonight?"

He nodded, the breeze ruffling his thick hair. "Sure. I thought we could take in The Gold Rush Boys."

Oh, man. The GRB was one of my favorite bar bands. "Are they at The Wooden Apple?" The Apple was a downtown nightclub with limited seating. It had a reputation for amazing bands and shows that went on long into the morning.

"Yep. I thought it might be fun. They're playing there tonight and coming back this weekend, but I know you're busy this weekend."

I started to agree then stopped to consider it. "How do you know I'm busy?"

He tugged his coat closed. "Can we talk about this over a beer and a plate of nachos? It's damn cold in this parking lot."

The nightclub was a public place. I would have my own car. The guy did rescue me from an evening with Aurora. "You mean it?"

"Sure. I got us a front row seat."

I eyed him with new respect. "How'd you do that?"

"Oh, I know a guy who knows a guy. Are you game?"

I ignored that nagging little voice in my head that said *this guy is too good to be real* and threw caution to the wind. "Why not?"

J L Wilson

Chapter 2

I followed behind Royal's dark brown SUV in my pickup truck to a parking garage downtown, pulling in next to him in the lot. He was waiting for me by the time I jumped down from the truck. "Nice wheels." He eyed my vintage black Chevy. "What year is it?"

"1997," I said. "Silverado. She only has sixty-k miles." I dropped the keys in my purse and walked with him out of the garage. "I got it new and somehow never got around to trading it in. I always used the company truck during the week, so that's why I have so few miles on it."

"Company truck?"

I ducked my chin into my coat collar. "Like you said—let's get someplace warm so we can talk."

He didn't push it, and I was grateful for that. The sellout of my store was still a sore point with me, and I wasn't anxious to hash it over. It didn't take us long to get to the Apple, a storefront on the ground floor of an office tower. We entered the bar side on the left. It was filled with patrons, some probably waiting for their tables at the restaurant side on the right.

Royal waded through the crowd. I followed in his wake to the bar, where he handed something to the bartender. The guy studied whatever it was then gestured to a waitress, who waved us to follow her. Royal thrust his arm out behind him. I took his hand, letting him break a path for me through the people sitting, standing, and shouting to be heard over the jukebox.

We ended up at a miniscule table at the edge of the dance floor, which was all that separated us from the small stage. He ordered a fancy beer and the nachos, and I got a tap beer. Several couples were already warming up with a line dance. I assessed the participants while we ordered drinks and food.

"I just learned to line dance recently," Royal confided, leaning against me to be heard. "I'm not very good at it yet."

"It takes practice," I conceded. "A lot depends on who takes the lead." He shot me a quizzical look. "Somebody always sets the tone and the steps when a line dance forms." I nodded to the people in front of us. "That girl in front is the lead. She's setting the line."

He eyed the girl, a tossed-hair brunette in skinny jeans and a red sweater with snowflakes positioned in just the right spots. She moved with assurance through the steps, the four people in her row and the four in the row behind her following her direction. "They must know the steps," he said.

"It's the song. There's a certain dance people do when 'Baby Likes To Rock It' is played."

One corner of his mouth twitched, and a dimple made an appearance. "I didn't recognize the song. That explains it. You folks all have a secret code."

"I guess you could say that. What kind of music do you normally listen to? I mean, if you don't recognize this one, then I'd have to guess country-western isn't your first choice."

"Oh, you know. Old classic rock." He glanced at

me as though gauging my reaction. "Show tunes."

I almost choked on my beer. "Show tunes?"

"Musical theater. I enjoy the story and the tunes. You know, shows like *Oklahoma*, or *My Fair Lady* or *Carousel*. I prefer the older ones, but some newer ones are good, too."

I considered that. The last time I went to a play was when I went to *The Nutcracker* to watch a friend's little kid play one of the mice. That little kid was now the mother of a toddler. "Well, that's interesting," I said, not quite sure what else to say. My acquaintance with musical theatre was brief and fleeting, at best. I decided to leave that topic for another time. "Tell me some more about yourself. What do you do for a living? Where do you live?"

"Like I said in my profile, I live on the west side of town, too." He sipped his beer and piled some chips on his plate along with a healthy dollop of guacamole and salsa. I noticed he avoided the clump of chips that were saturated with so-called cheese. Good. More for me. "It's smart that our addresses don't show up in the app. Safer that way for everybody."

"Yeah, that's great." I made a mental note to download the app and start familiarizing myself with it. I also needed to get my account information from Vaughan, bless his pointy little head. Lord knows what he put in my profile.

"I guess I wasn't one-hundred-percent up-front with my information." He regarded me warily. "I mean, I said I was a consultant, but I didn't say what kind."

I extracted a cheese-laden bunch of chips and maneuvered them onto my own plate along with a generous helping of taco meat. "I figured business analyst or something like that." I hoped that made sense with whatever he had written.

"Well, kind of. I work with the police."

I stared at him, a loaded corn chip poised halfway to my mouth. "What? You're a cop?"

"No, I'm not with the local police. I just advise them." He sipped his beer then set his glass down very carefully before tilting his head to regard me from under his dark eyelashes. "Is that a problem?"

I bit into the corn chip to give me time to think. "Do you carry a gun and handcuffs and all that stuff?" I eyed his jacket, which I suppose was loose enough to hide a firearm. The only cops I'd seen besides Finn were on TV. It seemed like they managed to carry an amazing amount of equipment on their person.

"Would it matter if I did?" He held my gaze as though daring me to find fault with his choice of profession.

"I don't know," I admitted. "I've never known anybody who worked in law enforcement. Isn't it kind of dangerous? Do you have to be around criminals and stuff?"

His mouth twisted in that wry half-smile I was coming to recognize. "Yeah, I don't associate with a better class of person if that's what you mean. But it's not all the time. Mostly it's paperwork and bureaucracy and office work. It's just now and then that I get into the field and get my hands dirty." He dished out more guacamole. "So to speak."

I scooped up another spoonful of cheesy goodness. "You didn't answer my question." I had to almost shout to be heard over the hoots and hollers of the audience, who were cheering the band as they took their place on the stage.

"Which one?" He leaned close to me so I could speak into his ear.

"Do you carry a gun?"

He straightened and nodded.

"Like, now?"

He held his jacket open, twisting so I could see the gun in the holster under his arm.

"Sholey hits," I breathed.

"Sholey what?" He let the jacket drop closed.

"Oh, it's a thing my father taught me." I took a swallow of beer. "I spent a lot of time around some tough landscape crews growing up. My father took me to job sites, and they often swore like crazy. He told me a lady shouldn't swear out loud, but if her words got jumbled, well—" I shrugged. "It happens. That's how I learned 'sholey hits' and 'foley huck' and 'teasus jits' and 'wass ipe'. I only use the real thing when I get big-time upset."

"Wass ipe?" Royal's lips framed the true expression, then he grinned. "I like it."

I nodded toward his coat. "So yeah—sholey hits. I've never seen a gun up close."

"Ask real nice, and I'll let you touch it." Royal winked then picked up his glass.

The band chose that moment to launch into "Watermelon Crawl," which filled the dance floor immediately. I was glad for the distraction because I wasn't quite sure how to handle that invitation of his. I focused on food and drink and came to realize that having a first date in a nightclub is a great idea. It's busy, so you don't have to focus too much on each other. It's loud, so you don't need to talk a lot except in little bits. And if you get bored, there are always other people to watch or music to hear.

In between dance tunes we exchanged bursts of information. I was hard pressed to make it sound plausible because in theory I had already reviewed his details. But I was able to glean that he was long divorced ('twenty years ago and change'), he had no pets ('I travel sometimes, so I've never felt right about having a dog or cat'), he had a condo in one of the newer loft-type buildings not far from downtown, he had an extensive cookbook collection, and he was two years away from mandatory retirement where he worked, although his boss might request a waiver to keep him on.

"Do you want to stay?" I had always been self-employed, so the intricacies of pension systems and their rules were foreign territory for me. "I mean, is it the kind of job you want to stick with for longer?"

"It's not really a question of do I want to do it." We were huddled over the table to talk and be heard over crowd noise, which was almost as loud as the band, who had taken a break. He was so close I could see his thoughtful, almost wistful, expression. "It's whether I can still do it or not. I can do the paperwork part of it, but the field work might get to be too much."

"That's okay, though, right? You would probably rather not have to be in the dangerous part of it all?" Even as I said it, something told me that being smack in the middle of the dangerous would be just what he'd like.

"It's not so much what I would like to do. When you work with law enforcement, it's all a team effort. I don't want to let the team down." He toyed with a chip, stabbing it into the remains of the guacamole. "When you let down the team, it might mean somebody's life."

Suddenly 'consultant to the police' sounded damn dangerous.

"What about you?" he asked. "You said something about a company car?"

"I used to co-own a business with my father," I said. "We just sold the property where the business sat, though, so I guess I'm retired now."

"Wait a minute. I read about that. You're part of the Dewitt sale, right? I mean, your business was. That landscaping company and store has been at that corner for years, hasn't it?"

"It was," I said glumly. "It's all being torn down as we speak. My father and mother started the business fifty years ago, right after I was born. I grew up in the landscape trade. I used to go with my father on job sites, helping him with designs and plant selections. When I got out of college, we started the gift store side of things. Now, though." I shrugged, trying to appear nonchalant. "I guess I'm retired."

"Where'd you go to college? I can't remember if it said on your profile."

"Oh, this tiny little college in upstate Minnesota. At one time I thought I'd go into geology, and they have a top-notch department. But I changed my mind halfway through and switched to Business Administration. I had an academic and an athletic scholarship."

"Really? A jock? What did you play—basketball?" He raked me up and down with green-eyed evaluation. "Somehow, I think not."

I laughed. "You'd be right. No, I had a golf

scholarship."

"Golf? Seriously? I didn't know they gave scholarships for golf."

"They sure do. Don't tell me. You played football, right? And probably basketball since you're so tall."

"Yep, you nailed it." Royal downed his beer then gestured to the waitress. She nodded, acknowledging the refill. "Do you stay in touch with any of your teammates? Is that what they call golf? A team?"

"It's a squad, and no, I haven't stayed in touch. That was a long time ago, in a galaxy far, far away." That reminded me. "You mentioned that you knew I'd be busy this weekend. How did you know that?"

"Your friend mentioned it. Vaughan, was that his name? He made some comment about your busy social calendar."

That sounded like something Vaughan would say. "Some friends of mine from college are coming for a visit. We get together every five years for a reunion."

"I guess that means you have stayed in touch with your squad-mates."

"No, not really. Charlene was on the same squad as me, but she passed on a few years ago. The others were all in different sports." I ticked the names off on my fingers. "Brian and Finn were in baseball, Paulina and Vaughan played tennis, Iven was on the rowing team, and Heidi played softball. She died last year." I took a last bite of corn chips and pushed my plate away. "We were Snow White and the Seven Jocks. That's what people called us. We all came from this part of Iowa. I guess we sort of bonded or something."

Royal grinned. "So instead of the seven dwarfs, you had—"

"Nimble, Sporty, Hopeful, Nerdy, Brainy, Bitchy, and Calm."

He laughed softly. "You have quite a bond if you're still getting together after all this time."

How much to tell him? I suppose it didn't matter. Besides, he worked with cops. It wouldn't shock him. "We went through sort of a traumatic time together. I think it really forged a friendship for us."

Royal smiled faintly. "Well, come on. You can't tease me like that. What happened?"

I checked the stage, but the band was still absent, so I had time to tell him at least some of the story. "It happened during our senior year, during the last semester." I swallowed some beer, my throat suddenly dry when memories began to crowd me. "I was in the locker room, getting ready to take a shower. A guy attacked me."

"What?" Royal's hand, resting on the table, suddenly clenched. "He—oh, my God, I'm sorry—did he assault you?"

"Almost. I mean, he did hit me, but he didn't manage to rape me. I screamed and fought him off. Finn and Vaughan were just coming in. The men's locker room was next to ours, and they heard me. They ran into the locker room and pulled the guy off me." I shot him a shaky smile. "It still freaks me out when I think about it."

Royal's hand closed over mine, and he squeezed gently. "I can understand why. That's horrible."

Most men couldn't understand the depth of fear that something like that left behind. But Royal was with the cops, so maybe he had a better understanding than most guys. "The attacker ran off, but I knew who he was. We all did. He worked in the athletic department. He was an assistant physical therapist who worked with the athletes on strength and conditioning. I reported it to the authorities, but back then nobody took that kind of thing seriously."

"What? That's crazy."

"That's how it was." It still angered me after all those years, but I no longer let it consume me. I took a deep breath. "The department didn't want a scandal. They claimed that I invited the guy to have some fun. When things got out of hand, I cried wolf. The fact that I had a black eye and bruises didn't mean anything."

"That's insane." Royal's green eyes seemed to sparkle with outrage. "Your friends were witnesses."

"Well, that's the problem, you see. Finn and Vaughan are gay. Back then, they couldn't admit that they'd been together because if anyone knew they were gay, they'd lose their scholarship. They didn't dare speak up. I know it really pissed them off, but that's how it was. They were in a bind. We all talked about it and that's when I found out that Sporty—Paulina— knew a girl who'd been attacked by the same guy."

"Damn. He'd done it before?" Royal's hand was still resting on mine. I was surprised how comforting it felt.

"He assaulted a girl on the softball team and one on the tennis squad. He got them drunk, one thing led to another, and he didn't take no for an answer. They were ashamed and afraid of reporting it. I mean, look what happened to me. They made me seem like a slut and a liar. How could those girls come forward, weeks after the fact, and hope to be believed?"

Royal leaned back, his hand slipping off mine. "It's

a fucked-up world, isn't it, when a woman is afraid to speak out about something like that?"

I had thought about this a lot over the years. "So many women are afraid to say no. They get into a situation and suddenly, it's all going too far, too fast. They feel guilty because they think that somehow they're to blame." I took another swallow of beer to wash away the bitterness. "That's how the police made me feel. There I was, the pretty little athlete in my shorts and knit shirt, walking around the rec center and flaunting myself. I wasn't, of course. Or maybe I was, but I sure wasn't trying to invite rape. For a time, I started to wonder if I was to blame or not."

"That's bullshit."

"That's how small-college cops thought thirty-some years ago. That's how a lot of people thought thirty-some years ago." I pushed an errant strand of hair back behind one ear, my hand shaking. "After that happened, we all stuck together. The guys made sure to escort us everywhere we went, and us girls never went into the locker room alone."

"What happened to the guy who attacked you?"

"Word got out. A couple of other girls came forward. Apparently, he had stalked them, sent them creepy notes, and hung around the practice field, watching them. A girl on the softball team was majoring in Women's Studies. She got her professors involved, telling them how our allegations were being blown off. It threatened to become an even bigger scandal because we weren't being treated fairly. The Athletic Department took the easy way out. They fired the guy. A few weeks after that, he was arrested for beating a girl on the tennis team. I testified at the trial and so did the other girls. He was convicted and sent to prison."

"Holy sh—I mean, sholey hits, what an experience."

I smiled. "Yeah, holy shit is right. I was twenty-one years old and so scared. But my father and my friends were there, supporting me, so I got through it. And that's why we all still get together every five years or so. Like I said, we have a bond that most people don't understand—lucky them."

"I can see why you stayed in touch." He swirled his beer in the glass, staring at the foam. "I know how that goes, kind of. I've stayed in touch with friends I went to post-graduate school with, too. Some experiences are intense. When do your friends get into town?"

"Sporty and Nimble got married and are coming in from Florida. Nerdy is coming from California. They're all due to arrive on Thursday night. They still have family around here and will spend some time with them. The other two live here in town. You've already met Hopeful—Vaughan. He and Calm live on the west side."

"The two gay guys? They're still together?"

I nodded. "Yep, Vaughan and Finn had a few bumpy years when Finn went off to the Army. Then he got out and went into more school. Hey, maybe you know him. Finn Sterling. He's a sheriff's deputy here in town."

"I may have met him," Royal said. "I've worked with quite a few people in the police and the sheriff's departments. It sounds like you'll be busy this weekend. I wonder…are you free on Thursday night?"

"Why? What do you have in mind?" I eyed his

jacket. "I'm not sure I'm ready to touch your firearm." I waggled my eyebrows, and he laughed.

"There's a play in town I'd like to go to. I thought maybe you'd like to go with me. I can get us tickets to *Showboat*. It's playing downtown at the Paramount. It's really a great production. I know the guy who's singing the part of Joe, and he's amazing. The woman playing Nolie is good, too. She can really hit the high notes."

Oh, Lord. Hit the high notes? It sounded like opera, which was a musical genre that made my teeth ache. Damn. I need to find a graceful way to decline. Sitting through a musical play would probably induce a coma. I began to marshal my excuses when I made the mistake of looking at him. Royal regarded me with a hopeful eagerness that totally squashed any thought I had of begging off. "Sure," I managed. "You can teach me all about musical theater. I can teach you about line dancing."

"Deal." He raised his glass of beer, and we clicked rims. "I have a lot to learn."

"I don't even know what I have to learn," I confessed. "Musical theater just isn't something I've experienced. Heck, any kind of theater is foreign territory for me."

"All you have to do is enjoy it. *Showboat* has a terrific story and, like I said, the principal players have great voices." He suddenly patted his coat then pulled a phone out of his inner pocket, eyeing the display. "I'm sorry. I need to take this call. Will you excuse me?"

"Sure. I'll save your seat." I watched him unfold from the chair and turn to go into the crowd. He had a nice, lean body, sort of long and angular. What an odd, complicated man—consultant to cops and connoisseur of musical theater. It had been a long time since I met anyone who was interesting. It seemed like I was usually getting hit on by a married man who wanted a diversion or someone who thought he was God's gift to poor, spinster lady me. Royal was neither and—

I realized I was thinking of him as 'Royal', not 'Brendan'. That was odd, but it seemed right, somehow. Before I could pursue that thought, I heard "Your Last Call," by Lee Ann Womack, blaring from my purse. That was my ringtone for a text message. When I dug it out and checked the screen I saw an icon for Cruella de Vil. It was the photo I had uploaded for my stepmother in my contact list.

"What does that bitch—" I glared at the message that appeared.

Lv yr fthr alne. You cant help.

"What the hell?" I started to fire back a response but before I could, a man slipped into Royal's vacant seat. "Hey, sorry. That seat's taken." I lowered the phone.

The man leaned close to me, his face just inches from mine. "I just wanted to say hello, Snow. It's been so long since I've seen you. I used to love visiting you."

I had repeat customers that I often passed on the street without recognizing them in the context of my shop. "I closed the store recently," I said. "I guess you missed out on the going-out-of-business sale."

"I missed out on so much since I've been gone." He tilted his head to one side, his gaze sweeping over my face. "You haven't changed. I'm sure I have, though." He leaned even closer.

I frowned, pulling back. His insistent closeness was unsettling. There was something about his eyes that was familiar, but I couldn't place where I knew him from. His face was squarish, with harsh lines around his mouth extending down from his eyes, so deep they were almost like scars. His light-colored hair was short, like a buzz cut, but longer in back. It was an odd style and one I was sure I'd remember. "I'm not sure I know where—" I glimpsed Royal working his way through the crowd to me.

The guy saw my attention shift and he jumped up, his hand landing on my shoulder. "Good to see you." He squeezed hard. I twisted away from the pain.

"Leave me alone." I was talking to empty space. The man wiggled through the crowd around the dance floor and was gone.

"Everything okay?" Royal asked, leaning over me.

I nodded. "Yeah. It was just some guy who thought he knew me." I shrugged.

"I hate to say this, but I have to cut our evening short. Something's come up. I need to check in at work. I'm sorry."

"That's okay," I assured him. "I understand." I stepped away from the table and gestured to a girl standing nearby. "It's all yours."

She grabbed my vacated chair and sat down, waving her friends to join her. I fell in behind Royal, and we elbowed our way to the front door, emerging to find sodden snow dropping down and turning to slush almost immediately. We jogged to the parking garage but by the time we got there, we were both shaking snow off our coats and hair. "Damn, I didn't see that in the forecast," I said while I dug my truck keys out of my purse.

"You know what they say: a weather forecast and a

buck will buy you coffee." Royal opened my truck door for me.

I stepped up on the running board. "Thanks for an interesting evening." I tossed my purse into the cab then turned. I was almost the same height as him, and it seemed natural to lean over and kiss his cold cheek.

"No, thank you for letting me cut it short. Can I make it up to you? How about going out for dinner tomorrow night?" Royal hunched his shoulders in his jacket, his breath blowing out in clouds. "Someplace warmer than this and quieter than a bar."

I laughed. "That sounds great. Where should I meet you?"

"I'll call you, and we'll figure it out." He pulled out his phone. "What's your number?" I recited it, and he typed it into his contact list. "Got it. I'll call you tomorrow." He leaned forward, and I met him halfway for a quick brushing of the lips. "Thanks, Snow."

I slid into the truck. "Talk to you later," I said as he closed the door.

"You can bank on it." He watched me back out then he went to his SUV. I exited the garage and when I went left onto 2nd Street he went right. I waved to him in the rear-view mirror. He honked before turning the corner.

I focused on my driving. The roads were sloppy and getting sloppier by the minute. It was okay in town where there had been some traffic. But when I got out to my neighborhood the snow was coming down heavier. In spots it was hard to see the edge of the road.

I hated driving at night in snow. There was just enough on the road to make it feel greasy, as though my truck was doing a slippery dance even though I was well below the speed limit. I took my time, maintaining a constant pace on the hills and valleys, my frozen hands clenching the steering wheel.

I spied my driveway coming up on the left at the bottom of the hill. I needed to slow to make the turn, so I let up on the gas, trusting that my momentum would get me there. As I did, a car's lights suddenly came on ahead of me. It must have been parked on the right side of the road, just past my driveway. I couldn't tell how close it was to my entry.

Then the car's lights switched to bright, and it moved toward me.

Chapter 3

Thank God for winter driving experience. I resisted the impulse to jerk the steering wheel to the right, knowing a deep ditch awaited me there. Instead I tapped the brakes and turned the wheel a tad bit to the left. As I expected, the downward momentum of the hill combined with the braking to make the truck fishtail slightly, slowing me enough that I could correct it to the right.

The car squeaked past me, accelerating to go up the incline. "Asshole!" I shouted. "Butthole jerk!" I checked the rear-view mirror but all I saw was the dark rear end of the sedan. This was not a well-traveled street, used mainly by the residents of the neighborhood. I didn't recognize the car, but I had just a glimpse before darkness and snow hid it from sight.

I made a cautious turn into my lane, which I had outlined with orange safety poles to show me the way. By the time I got to my house, my pulse was under control again. I consoled myself with the thought that had I been in an accident, at least it would have been close to home. Small comfort, perhaps.

As I rounded the turn, I saw the light on in my workshop downhill a few steps from my house. I pulled into the attached garage and debated: go check the shop through the snow or go inside?

I knew if I went into the house without checking,

I'd worry about the shop all night. With a sigh, I closed the garage door and hung my purse on the railing to the step leading inside. I left through the side door nearest to my shop, the motion light clicking on to show me the way. I went to the four steps leading down a slight slope. The workshop door was closed but not locked.

I *always* locked it. When was the last time I was in here? I paused while I considered that. It was on Monday afternoon, when I got the last of the items to sell that I had stored in here. I loaded up my truck and drove to the consignment store that would handle the remnants of my store goods.

I pushed open the door and went in. It wasn't until I'd gone a step or two that I realized I probably should be cautious. What if someone was inside? As soon as the thought came, I dismissed it. I would have seen tire tracks in the snow outside if anyone had been on my lane, and my car was the first to leave tracks. Reassured, I stepped in.

My studio was a big open space with two workbenches against the far walls and one in the center, where a car would normally park. Windows at the back faced the woods behind the house, unseen in the dark.

I went to the workbench where my latest sculpture sat. It was mostly metal, composed of bits of hardware, a random spoon or part of a fork, and anything bright and shiny that caught my eye. My tools—welding torch and snippers—were where I left them on Sunday when Vaughan and I talked.

I started to go, but something didn't feel right. I turned back to peer at the workbench. I had sorted through some items to include—a couple of old metal toys, bits of a roller skate including its key, odd-shaped refugees from a hardware bin. They were arrayed on my work surface in plastic containers with small dividers to sort things easily. I stared at the open containers, but nothing seemed obviously wrong.

I shivered when a sharp wind blew into the room, the door scraping over the snow I tracked in. It was too cold and too late to prowl around here tonight. I would inspect things more closely in the morning. I shut off the light and made sure the lock was set, then left the building, pulling the door firmly closed behind me.

My footprints on the steps outside were already filling with sloppy snow. I trudged up the slope and into my attached house garage, kicking off my boots to rest on the heated mat outside the house door. I just got inside when I heard my landline phone ringing. I saw the kitchen clock, illuminated by the light I left on over the stove. It was almost midnight. Who would be calling?

My answering machine kicked on, but no one left a message. I shrugged out of my jacket, stowing it in the closet on my right. Mr. Gold sauntered into the kitchen, pausing near his food bowls to confirm that nothing miraculous had occurred while he napped. Nope, only kibble was there. He peered up at me mournfully.

"Sorry, kid." I bent over to rub his ears. "Chow time is over."

"Friends in Low Places" chimed from my purse, signaling a friend was calling. I dug out my phone. Vaughan's picture showed on the display. "Hey, you," I said answering it. "What's so urgent?"

"Where have you been? Are you okay?"

"Of course, I'm okay. I was with Mr. Right Now, remember?"

"You shouldn't just go off with a stranger." Vaughan sounded almost panicked. "What if he turned out to be a pervert or something?"

"Hey, you're the one who set me up with him. You're the one who said that dating site was totally safe." I wandered into the living room to stare at the snow falling outside.

"It is, but that's not why I'm calling. Sporty and Nimble had a break-in at their house in Florida. She called me earlier tonight. They were at some banquet thing. They came home and found out somebody had broken in and smashed up Nimble's trophy case and vandalized their kitchen and I don't know what-all."

"Foley huck, that's terrible." I sank down on my couch, tucking my legs under me. The windows faced the woods behind the house. Even though it was night, there was ghostly whiteness of snow outlining my deck and the shape of the picnic table at the far end of my yard. The weather made the world appear like a camera negative. "Was anything taken?"

"They're still assessing the damage, I would imagine. It was just a few hours ago. Sporty called us as soon as the police left. She wanted to talk to Finn about it."

That made sense, I suppose. Finn was a deputy with the sheriff's department. Whenever I had a law enforcement question, I, too, checked with Finn first. That reminded me. "Before I forget—Mr. Right Now works with the police. Ask Finn if he knows him."

There was a dense pause, then Vaughan said, "Sure, I will. Can you imagine? I mean, I know Nimble and Sporty live in the high rent district, and I suppose they're a target for a robber, but wouldn't that be awful?"

"Are they still coming on Thursday?"

"Sporty said they're planning on it unless something happens that they need to stay in town because of this."

My landline phone rang again. "Hold on. Somebody's calling me."

"Who's calling you this late at night?" Vaughan demanded.

"Good question." I reached for the phone, sitting on the end table next to the couch. I didn't recognize the phone number on the small LED. "I don't know who it is. I'm not answering," I told Vaughan. "And it's late so I'm going to sleep."

"How was your date? You can't leave me in suspense like this. Was it okay? Is he Mr. Right?"

I laughed. "I'll talk to you tomorrow, Vaughan. Good night." I hung up before he could pepper me with questions again and put the phone on the wireless charging pad sitting on the side table. As I did, I saw the display of my landline phone. It was on the third ring and kicking over to the message machine. I waited, listening. Then I heard a faint voice. "Good night, Snow."

Something in the tone of voice was furtive, chilling. I remembered my shop and the door I thought I'd locked. I sprang to my feet and went to the kitchen door, making sure it was locked. Then I dashed downstairs, verifying that the door leading to the patio was locked, too. I raced back upstairs as though the Boogey Man was after me, startling Miss Copper into a run for the bedroom.

My mobile phone played Lady A's "Hello, World,"

my general-purpose ringtone. I eyed it warily. I didn't recognize the number, but it was a local call. I let it go to voice mail, not sure I wanted any more Boogey Men in my life right now. When the voice mail icon lit up, I checked it.

"Hi, Snow. It's Brendan Royal. I wanted to check and make sure you got home okay. The roads are a bit slippery out there, and I just wanted—you know. To make sure you're okay. I'll call you tomorrow, I guess."

I tapped the *Call* icon. Royal answered on the first ring. "Thanks for calling me back. The roads were pretty bad, so I thought I'd check and make sure you didn't have any problems."

I sat back. What a nice feeling, knowing somebody was checking in on me. "Sure, I'm fine. The roads were lousy, but I took my time."

"I felt like such a jerk. I should have at least volunteered to follow you, to make sure you got home safely. But something came up and I had to—and you know, now that I think about it, maybe that would have been creepy to have me follow you."

I laughed. "I suppose it does sound creepy, but I know you have the best of intentions."

There was a short pause. "Well, I have intentions." His voice was definitely huskier. I shivered at the implications I thought I heard. "I guess we'll find out if you think they're good. I know it's late, so I'll let you go. I'll call you in the morning, and we'll figure out where to go for dinner."

"Okay, that sounds good. Thanks for checking on me."

"This whole evening was my pleasure. Good night, Snow." His warm voice caressed my name, and I shivered again.

"Good night, Royal." I tapped the *Off* icon. His phone number was displayed. I decided, why not take a chance? I stored Royal's phone number and for his ringtone I chose "Cowboy, Take Me Away" by the Dixie Chicks. Maybe I was tempting fate, but something told me I had a winner there.

Only time would tell for sure.

I checked my door locks one more time then fell into bed and a dreamless sleep. When I awoke I discovered an inch or so of snow had fallen overnight, but the driveway appeared just wet. I breathed a sigh of relief. I wasn't anxious to break out my snow blower yet.

I did my usual two-mile run on the treadmill downstairs followed by a short weight workout with one of the many DVDs I'd accumulated over the years. I was showered and driving to Roy's house by seven-thirty.

My old family home was about halfway between what used to be our westside business location and our eastside one, north of town. It used to be in the country but was now part of suburbia. The two-story white frame house sat back from the road, Roy's truck in the driveway in front of the two-car garage. I frowned when I saw it. Why wasn't it in the garage? Aurora drove a Honda sedan, and there was ample room for Roy's truck alongside her car. No need for it to sit out and get snow-covered.

Aurora had gone on a decorating spree a year or so ago. The house was no longer the serene place I remembered from childhood. The shiny hardwood floors were replaced with thick green carpet, the couch was now a bright burgundy, not a muted brown-and-gold, and Roy's shabby recliner had been relegated to a back room. An overstuffed armchair in a bright burgundy-and-gold pattern took its place. The coffee table had disappeared. Now a big hassock was there with a tray positioned on the middle. The glass-topped end tables were gone, replaced by round white tables that I thought were hideous with the furniture.

Every room had a mirror of some kind in it, which I suppose spoke to Aurora's vanity. I hadn't been upstairs since Roy married Aurora, but I imagined it was as changed as the downstairs. Aurora had warned me of the impending changes and asked if I wanted any of the old furniture before she had it hauled away. I was surprised that she even considered my feelings in the matter. I eagerly took a small dresser and desk that I remembered from my childhood. They now sat in my downstairs family room.

Even the kitchen was remodeled, with white countertops replacing the old faux wood laminate, black trim around everything making the shapes stand out in sharp relief. All the clutter was gone from the surfaces, with the small appliances tucked into some cabinet or cupboard. The overall effect was sterile and spotless, a contrast to the messy clutter that Roy and I used to have when I lived there.

The house even smelled differently, something I noticed every time I went there. A pervasive, faint pine aroma seemed to be constantly in the air. I never noticed any indication that people lived there—no food smells, or a fresh breeze from the outside, or a whiff of Aurora's perfume. Just that suggestion of pine, as though the house was in a state of continual cleanliness.

My father was at the front curtain, peeking out. He pulled open the front door as soon as I got out of my truck. "We don't have much time." He gestured frantically to me to get into the house. I scurried as fast as I dared on the slippery sidewalk and ducked inside, Roy closing the door behind me with a slam. "Come in here." He went left, into what used to be his home office. Now it was a sitting room of some sort, his old wooden desk replaced with two green love seats angled to face an upright piano in the corner on the right.

"Since when did you play piano?" I pulled off my jacket and dropped it on an arm of one of the love seats.

"She plays." Roy went to the window and peered anxiously outside. "She'll be back soon from the gym. I need to talk to you before she comes back." He turned to face me, giving me my first good look at him. His hair, white and thick, was matted on one side, and he appeared bent slightly, as though he was hunching his shoulders.

"Nice outfit," I said with a grin.

His head dropped to his red plaid sweatpants, pink T-shirt, and bright green cardigan that was buttoned haphazardly. Bright blue high-top sneakers completed the ensemble. "She makes me wear it. She took away all my other clothes. She wants me to stay inside." He pulled me to him. "I'm so glad you came. I've been wanting to talk to you, but I can't because she's always around. She's always watching me."

I squeezed him tightly, surprised at how thin and fragile his bones felt. I remembered Roy as being robust and strong, but this was a frail, old man in my arms. "I know." I pulled away to smile at him. "Aurora likes to stick by you. I'm surprised she goes away to the gym and leaves you here alone."

Roy put his finger to his lips. "Don't tell her," he said with a twinkle in his eyes. "I pretend to take the pills she gives me. She thinks I'm sound asleep upstairs, but sometimes I spit out the pill, so I can stay awake."

"What? She's giving you pills?" This was the first I'd heard of any ill health on his part, but admittedly, I'd been segregated from his life since his marriage.

He waved that away. "The doctor told me I need to get more rest. I only take them now and then. I'm so glad you came over. I've been wanting to talk to you about the sale. I didn't want to do it, you know. Aurora thought we should sell because she thought it was getting to be too much for me."

Roy grasped my hands tightly. His were as cold as ice and still callused and slightly crippled from arthritis. He had spent decades working alongside the manual laborers who installed his landscape designs, maneuvering heavy equipment, applying fertilizers and pesticides, manipulating rocks and paving materials into gardens. His hands reflected his life's work.

"There's no reason you have to keep doing it," I said reassuringly. "You can take it easy if you want to."

"She thought I couldn't manage the business anymore. She might make me sell it completely."

Damn. I didn't want to get into this with him. In the past five years or so, he had been losing his touch when it came to the business side of things. Several small mishaps occurred like lost invoices or bills not paid. I attributed it to his distractions because of his marriage. It was so typical of Aurora to put the blame on him.

"There's nothing wrong with retirement," I said when I saw his anxious eyes. "I think you could trust Paul Minster to handle things." Paul had worked with Roy for decades and knew the business inside and out. Having him take over would be the same as keeping it in the family.

Roy released my hands and stepped back. "I won't let him have it. I won't. I don't trust Paul to run things the way they should be run."

I had been out of the loop on the landscaping side of things for a long time. "Well, you don't have to sell or retire unless you want to." I slipped my arm through his. "Let's have a cup of coffee and talk about it."

"We don't have time." Roy glanced at the front window. "She'll be back soon." His dark eyes were wide with worry. "I feel like she's choking me sometimes."

I wanted to laugh at his dramatic words, but he was so worried I didn't. "What do you mean?"

"She's choking me off from everybody. She never invites you here. I never see any of my old friends. Why won't she let me see them?"

I had my thoughts about that. I suspected his friends just wouldn't feel welcomed in this new sterile home Aurora had made. "Maybe you need to make new friends, friends that you share with her. You've started a new life with her, so maybe new friends are okay." I confess, I felt a small measure of spiteful satisfaction saying that. I had been eliminated from his life. Let him and his new wife make a new life together.

"But I miss you so much," he muttered. "I miss my life." He picked anxiously at a loose button on the sweater. "She's trying to control everything. Well, I'm still in control of some things. I changed my will. She's not going to get anything."

I was pretty sure that wasn't going to happen because they had signed a pre-nuptial agreement. I knew for a fact she would get at least fifty-percent of anything he owned. I didn't bother pointing that out now, though. I just said, "I'm sure it's all just a misunderstanding or something. She just wants what's best for you."

"That's what she says but I don't believe her. I think she's trying to—" We both turned when we heard the garage door opening. "She's coming home. You need to leave." Roy dragged me to the front door. I barely had a chance to grab my jacket before he opened the door and thrust me outside.

I almost ran over Aurora, who was reaching for the door handle. She wore navy blue sweatpants and a matching fleece jacket. Her blonde hair was pulled back into a ponytail, and I swear she was wearing makeup. Who wears makeup to the gym?

"Snow—it's nice to see you. I didn't know you were coming over for a visit." She moved past me to the house. "Roy, you didn't mention that Snow was coming."

I stepped aside, pulling on my coat. "I just felt like dropping by."

"That was nice of you." Aurora went to Roy, who clung to the open door. "Look at you. That's my sweater, you silly man. Let me fix that." She laughed softly and reached for the mis-buttoned cardigan.

Roy shrunk back, away from her. "I'm fine. I don't need your help." He whirled, stumbling away into the house.

Aurora smiled frostily at me. "Good to see you." She shut the door firmly in my face.

I hesitated, my finger poised over the doorbell. Then I gave a mental shrug. Dad and Aurora were the picture of happiness last night. Maybe they had a fight or something and this was Dad's way of venting. I'd call him later in the day and see if they made up. Maybe I'd also check in with Paul Minster at the eastside store. They would be gearing up for the big holiday season. I could stop in and see how things were going.

I spent the morning running errands, swinging by my favorite deli for a salad for lunch. I didn't get home until early afternoon, by which time I was on the west side of town. Any thought of going to the east side to talk to Paul had vanished. I stopped on the street for my mail then went to my shop and started sorting through the bits and pieces I was considering for my sculpture. I was only there for a few minutes when I heard a car pull into the drive.

I went to the shop door as Vaughan was getting out of his SUV. To my surprise, Finn Sterling, Vaughan's husband, was with him. "Hey, guys. What are you doing out my way?"

"I was telling Finn about your hot date last night." Vaughan winked at me then went inside. He and Finn were both dressed in jeans and denim jackets, which told me that neither was on duty.

Finn followed Vaughan into the shop, and I closed the door behind us. "Any more news about Sporty and Nimble?" I asked him. "Are they still planning to come out?"

Finn paused when he saw my golf clubs lying on one of the tables. "You're late getting the clubs put away."

"Heck, it was warm enough last week I played a round. But I think it's time to clean 'em up and call it quits."

Finn inspected my nine-iron, which needed new wrapping on the shaft. "I talked to Nimble this morning. He said they were catching the morning flight."

"Don't keep us in suspense," Vaughan said. "How did the date go?" He went to my sculpture workbench and started poking around the items I had laid out.

"Stop that," I said. "I have it all sorted."

"Yeah, right. Come on, quit stalling. How did the date go?"

"It was nice," I admitted. "I'm sorry we had to cut the night short because he had work stuff to do."

Finn ambled over to join Vaughan. He was tall and slender, with thinning blond hair and pale blue eyes. "It can be tough to date somebody in law enforcement. There are a lot of interrupted dinners."

"He's not really in law enforcement. He's a consultant or something."

Finn regarded me with that deadpan expression of his that had earned him the nickname Calm. "Even consultants can be called out at all hours. All I'm saying is you need to keep that in mind if you're going to be seeing him."

I waved that off. "We'll cross that bridge later. Do you know him? He said he might know you. Brendan Royal?"

"Yeah, I think so. Big guy? Tall? White hair?" Finn leaned over my workbench, eyeing the pile of metal junk there. He nudged a few around, a couple of loose bits clinging to his knit gloves.

"That's him," I confirmed. "What does he do?"

"Do?"

"He said he was a consultant. What does he do?"

Finn poked through the little pile of nuts and bolts, separating them into piles. "He's with a group that advises the police department sometimes."

"Advises them on what?"

He held up something. "What is this?"

I peered at it. "I don't know."

"It's a ring." Vaughan peeked around Finn's shoulder.

"It's not mine. I don't know where it came from." I reached for the ring, but Finn moved away. "I wonder if…nah, that's too silly."

"What's too silly?" Finn examined the ring in his gloved hand.

"When I came home last night, the shop was unlocked, and the lights were on. You don't suppose somebody came in and left this ring? Why would anybody do that?"

"What?" Finn lowered the ring and stared at me, his pale blue eyes alert.

"I came home, and the shop was unlocked and the light was on," I repeated. "I was pretty sure I locked things up when I left, but—"

"And you didn't call the police?" Finn demanded.

I shrugged. "Nothing appeared taken, so I didn't bother."

Vaughan was bent over the ring Finn still held, and now he straightened. "That's Sporty's ring. It's the championship ring they got when they won that tournament. I remember because it's got her initials on it and it was such a pretty red stone in the ring." He pointed at the ring. "See—P.A.C. We always made fun of her initials. We called her Pac Woman, remember? She and I played mixed doubles in that tournament. We came in second because of a bad call from a line judge. The guy was terrible." He grinned at me. "Some losses you never forget."

I elbowed him aside to get closer to Finn. "That's ridiculous. Why would I have Sporty's ring?"

Finn held up the ring between two gloved fingers. "Did you touch this?"

"Touch it? I didn't even know it was there."

Finn pulled a plastic bag out of his pocket and dropped the ring into it. "I think I'm going to have this checked."

"For what?" I laughed. "Come on, Finn. It's just a stupid joke or something."

He eyed me. "Humor me."

"Cowboy, Take Me Away" chimed from my cell phone sitting on the workbench. I snatched it up but not before Vaughan saw Royal's name on the display. "Ooh, a special ringtone," he said. "It must be serious."

"Shut up, Hopeful," I snapped. "Hello?" I said into the phone.

"Hi, is this a good time to talk?" Royal asked.

"It's a perfect time to talk," I said, eyeing Finn. "I've got Finn Sterling here, acting like a cop. Maybe you can interpret him for me."

There was a pause. "Okay," Royal said cautiously. "I can try."

"What does it mean when a cop takes out a little plastic bag and drops something in it?"

Finn held out his hand. "Let me talk to him."

"This is my phone call." I put the phone behind my back. "Hey!"

Vaughan pried the phone out of my fingers and handed it to Finn. "Be my guest."

"That's my call!" I protested.

Finn twisted away from me. "Back away, Snow. This is police business."

Chapter 4

I stumbled, startled by Finn's harsh voice. "What is it? What's wrong?"

He was listening to something then he held out my phone. "Talk to your friend. I'll deal with this."

"Wait a minute, Finn. What's going on?"

"Talk to your friend."

I put the phone to my ear. "Can you tell me what's going on?"

"Deputy Sterling is just being cautious," Royal said.

"But it's a stupid, I don't know, a stupid joke or something."

"Okay," Royal said in a confiding tone of voice, "it's something cops have to do. Any time we see something that seems suspicious, we need to check into it."

I watched Finn examine the ring through the plastic of the bag. It made sense, I suppose. Finn was one of the most conscientious people I knew. I once saw him jot down a license plate number of a speeding car while we were walking into a football game. "Okay, I guess. I still think it's a waste of time."

"Probably," Royal said. "But it's his time, so let him waste it. Now for the reason I called—where do you want to eat tonight? I was thinking we could go to The Treehouse."

"Oh, man, you must be reading my mind. I saw a story about it in the paper, and I've been wanting to try it. Do you think we can get in?" The Treehouse was one of the newest restaurants in town, situated at the edge of a park that was above a reservoir. The restaurant appeared suspended in space, the dining room cantilevered over the water.

"I think I can get us a seat. I know a guy who knows a guy."

I laughed. "You're a useful person to know. Now I can say I know a guy who knows a guy. What time?"

"Six o'clock? And I got us tickets for tomorrow night. The play starts at seven, so maybe we can get a bite to eat beforehand. There's a little bistro attached to the theater where we can get drinks and appetizers. How does that sound?"

"Wow. Dinner, two nights in a row. I'll be spoiled."

"My pleasure." His voice caressed the words, and I smiled at the implication. "Do you want to meet me at the restaurant, or should I pick you up?"

I hesitated. My house was isolated out here in the country, and I barely knew the guy. Of course, if Finn vouched for him, it was probably okay.

"Why don't we meet halfway," I said, thinking out loud. "I have to talk with the manager at my father's eastside store. The restaurant is kind of south of there. You could meet me, and I'll leave my car there while we're at the restaurant."

"That sounds like a plan," Royal said. "That's the nursery and landscape place out on Highway 7, right?"

"Yep, that's it."

"Okay, I'll be there at five-thirty."

"Great. See you then."

I breathed a sigh of relief. I didn't want to imply that I didn't trust him, but...

"Smart move." Vaughan nodded approvingly. "You can't be too careful."

Finn was staring at the sculpture on my workbench, his head tilted to one side. "What do you think?" I asked.

"I don't know," he said slowly. "I like it but I'm not sure why."

I slapped his arm. "No, I meant about Royal."

Finn finally shifted his attention to me. "His name is Brendan."

I nodded. "And I think of him as Royal."

"Your Prince Charming," Vaughan said smugly. "I told you."

"You're an incurable romantic," I said. "He's not Prince Charming. He's Mr. Right Now."

Finn looked from me to Vaughan. "I'm sure there's a reasonable explanation there someplace, but I'm not going to ask for it now." He ambled toward the door, pausing at a photograph I had on the workbench near the window.

"Is that why you guys came out? To find out about my date?"

Vaughan put an arm around my shoulders and gave me a squeeze. "That and moral support. You were a bit stressed last night at your father's party."

I sighed and walked with him to the door. "It's just so odd to see him with Aurora. I want to be happy for him, but I'm not sure she's what he needs now."

Finn opened the outside door. "It doesn't matter if she's what he needs. She's what he's got. You need to get used to it."

He was right, but I didn't want to hear it. "Yeah, sure," I said grumpily.

Vaughan gave me a little shake. "Buck up, Princess. Now that your Prince Charming is in your life, you'll be too busy to worry about your father." He kissed me quickly on the cheek and followed Finn to the SUV in my drive. "I'll call you tomorrow to get the update on your date tonight."

"You're a nosy old gossip." I laughed at Finn's bemused look. "You can call, but I won't dish any details."

"We'll see." Vaughan slipped into the SUV.

Finn tapped the pocket holding the plastic bag. "I'll let you know if we find out anything. Be careful, Snow. I worry about you out here alone."

The nearest house was across the road, almost a quarter-mile away. I had always loved my solitude, but Finn's words gave me a little shiver of disquiet. "It'll be okay, Calm. I'll make sure to double-check my doors. If I get spooked, I'll give you guys a call."

"Do that. I can be here in twenty minutes. If you get really spooked, call 911. They can get here in five."

"Will do." I watched him climb into the SUV, and I waved while they drove off.

I returned to the shop, but any creative energy I had was dissipated by Finn's odd behavior. I went into the house and took a quick nap, then showered and considered my wardrobe. I settled on black pants, a black sweater with red and white snowflakes, and my black leather coat. I fed the cats and left the house, making sure all doors were locked and lights were on or off as needed.

I drove to the eastside store, which was the original business that my father and mother started decades before. There were two buildings, one that held pots, gardening tools, and plants in season. The other served as a landscape design studio for my father and the other designers on staff.

I parked between the two buildings, glad to see that the store building had several cars in front. The store stocked holiday-themed merchandise, which kept it busy through Christmas. Usually the only lag time was in January, which I thought of as 'post-holiday blues and pre-gardening anticipation' time. Once February rolled around and those garden catalogs started to arrive in homes, people would begin to shop again.

I went into the design building. It was an open space with several offices in the interior. Large tables were set out near the windows, giving clients a better view of the plans for their locations. Most of the staff was seasonal so I wasn't surprised to see just a couple of guys there. Paul Minster, our eastside design foreman, was standing at one of the windows, staring down at a design spread out on the table in front of him.

Paul had worked for my family since getting out of the Landscape Design program at the tech college almost twenty years earlier. He was a gifted landscaper because he took time to listen to clients and assess what would truly fit their personalities and patience. He smiled when he saw me. "It's been a while since we've seen you out here, Princess. How are you doing?"

I joined him at the table, giving him a quick hug. Paul wasn't much taller than me with a solid, athletic build. He was possibly the handsomest man I'd ever met with thick dark hair, a ready smile, and expressive brown eyes. I think almost every woman client fell a little bit in love with him, and maybe a few male clients did, too. "I'm doing okay, Paul. Getting used to not going in to work every day."

He sighed. "I was sorry to see your dad sell the land, but it made sense. He's getting older, and it was too hard to keep up with the work."

I studied the design on the table to cover my surprise. This was the first I'd heard of any problems with Roy handling the workload. However, I had only a peripheral involvement in that part of the business, so I suppose it was possible.

The plan in front of me was of a large residential property, and it was in the preliminary stages. When a designer worked on a design, he usually started with existing structures and features then overlaid it with successive sheets of thin paper euphemistically called bumwad. That let a person try out different ideas without committing to a final plan.

Each designer had a unique way of drawing standard elements such as trees, shrubs, buildings, and the hardscape of driveways and sidewalks. I recognized my father's distinctive handwriting on some of the descriptions, but most of the design was done in Paul's tidy, precise writing. "This is a big project. New house?" I picked up the large watercolor painting that showed a three-story house sitting atop a hill.

"Yeah, it's in a development on the north side of town. The developer wanted us to do several of the model homes. They'll break ground in the spring. He wants us to have the designs ready to go." Paul frowned at the plans.

"That's a big contract. It'll keep you busy next

year."

"If we get it." Paul shook his head. "Your father met with them last week to go over our preliminary ideas, but he wasn't ready. It didn't go very well."

"Really? What happened?"

Paul went to the break area in the middle of the room, away from the design tables. That was a firm rule—no food or beverages near the tables. I followed him, taking a seat while he poured himself a cup of coffee from the never-ending coffeepot. "Aurora drove him to the meeting." Paul slipped into the seat next to me. He glanced around, but the two other staff members were at the far end of the space, studying a plan on one of the tables. "She showed up with him and tried to intrude on the meeting."

"What? That makes no sense. She doesn't know beans about landscaping." I studied Paul's worried face.

"That's not the first time. He missed an appointment a month ago then he missed another one a week or so after that. I was able to cover for him, but— he's losing his touch, Snow. It's like he's lost interest in the business."

I sat back, my mind awhirl. "Maybe it's because of her," I said slowly. "He's probably distracted. We had the sale to get through and closing the store and the business on the west side. Maybe he's just been overworked."

"Maybe." Paul said doubtfully. "But, well, it seems like it's been getting worse for the past couple of years."

"Since he married Aurora. That's what you mean, right?"

Paul nodded. "I suppose. That development project

is a big one. It's going to take all my time. I think we need to hire another designer, maybe two, to pick up the slack. I figured we'd use the guys who used to work at the westside store, but Roy said he wasn't sure he wanted to. I said that they were good guys, they knew the business. Why not just use them? But Roy got angry and said that he'd handle whatever needs to be done." Paul stared into his coffee mug, his face troubled. "I don't think he can, though. When I asked him about it a week or two later, he said sure, we should use the guys from the old store and get them on board and going. It's like he forgot we even talked."

"That's odd." I remembered several conversations Roy and I had when the subject came up months earlier. "I was under the impression he planned to keep those designers on if they wanted the work. Do you want me to talk to him? I hate to see the business suffer because of Aurora."

Paul tilted his head to regard me, a faint smile making his dimples appear. "She's quite a distraction for him, isn't she? She's a distraction for a lot of people."

"What do you mean?" I checked over my shoulder. We were away from the others in a private little area. His cheeks darkened with color, and suddenly I understood. "Did she make a pass at you? Did she?"

"It was weird," he said, his voice pitched so low I had to lean closer to hear him. "She asked me to come out to the house one day early in the summer. There was a problem with their irrigation system, and she couldn't figure it out. I told her that Roy could fix it, but she insisted that I come out and evaluate it. When I got there, she was in a swimsuit and, well, that swimsuit left nothing to my imagination." He frowned, and I saw his confusion. "She was all over me while I worked on the system—it was just clogged and needed to be snaked—and then Roy came out. He was home the whole time. I thought he was at the westside store, but he was there. When he saw us, he got mad and told me to leave."

"I never heard about this. What happened after that?"

"I came back here then later in the day I went to the westside store to talk to Roy. He acted like nothing had happened. Said there wasn't any problem with the irrigation system and thanks for coming out but everything's fine." Paul shook his head, frowning. "He told me that he went home for lunch and that's why he was there. But I was there in the morning not at lunchtime. The clerk at the store told me Roy often didn't come in until afternoon. That explains why he missed some meetings, I guess."

"That is weird." This was the first I'd heard of any odd behavior. "I wonder if I should talk to him about it." Even as I spoke I wondered how I would broach such a subject.

Paul put his hand over mine on the table. "Thanks, but I'll handle it. We have some time before this project really heats up. I talked to the guys who will work here. They'll start in January. Maybe by then—"

"Snow?"

I looked up. Royal stood a few feet away, watching us. His dark gray overcoat was open, showing his dark gray jeans and black sweater over a white shirt with a striped necktie. It was a casually sexy style. He seemed surprised or maybe puzzled. I couldn't quite interpret his expression.

"Right on time." I pushed back from the table. "Brendan Royal, this is Paul Minster." I stood and so did Paul, reaching out to shake Royal's hand. "We planned to meet here," I told Paul. "I'll leave my truck in the lot and pick it up later."

Paul winked at me. "Make sure to take the keys. You know I like that truck."

I waggled a finger at him. "Don't you dare mess with my wheels." I gave him a quick hug. "Let me know if I can help at all," I said softly.

He nodded. "Thanks, Snow. It's good to know you're still part of the business." He nodded to Royal then went back to the design table.

Royal and I left the building. "Did you need more time to talk?" Royal asked while we walked toward his SUV parked next to my truck.

"No, that's okay. I might give him a call later to follow up on some details." I slid into the passenger seat when Royal opened the door for me, my mind churning through what Paul said. I had talked to Roy about the people who worked at the westside location before it closed. He assured me all of them would be offered jobs. It made no sense for him to not use good designers, especially if what Paul said was true. They had some big jobs in the future. They would need all hands on deck.

Royal got in and turned to me. "Is everything okay? That seemed like a pretty serious conversation." He started the car, backing slowly out of the parking spot.

"It's all just business stuff." I stared at the building in front of us, envisioning my father inside, working on a design plan. I had spent so many hours with him, watching him put down on paper the ideas that became beautiful landscapes. It was hard to imagine him not doing that anymore. If what Paul said was true, maybe it was time for Roy to walk away. I sighed, fighting a surge of anger at the thought of Aurora inserting herself into Roy's work.

"Are you sure everything's okay? I thought I might be interrupting something."

Royal was staring straight ahead, focused on the road. "With Paul? Nah, he and I have known each other for years. No, we were just talking about work."

Royal's shoulders, which had been hunched, relaxed. "Oh, okay. Good. It seemed like, well, you know, like…"

"He's ten years younger than me and happily married," I said. "But thanks for that boost to my ego."

Royal glanced at me then resumed his study of the road. "You're a beautiful woman," he said, his voice soft. "It wouldn't surprise me if some young guy was interested in you."

"Thanks," I said. "I appreciate the compliment."

We rode in silence for a few minutes then I said, "Did you talk to Finn after he left my house? I was wondering about that ring he found."

"No, I didn't."

"I still think Finn overreacted. I've been thinking about it. I wonder if I had that ring and just forgot I had it. I was going through a bunch of junk in my jewelry box and maybe I had it. Although why I'd have Sporty's ring, I don't know."

Royal didn't answer immediately. "I suppose it does feel like he's blowing it out of proportion, but that's just how cops are. We're trained to see things in different ways than most people do. When a cop finds something unusual, it just bugs him until he can figure it out."

"But what's to figure out? It's just some prank or misunderstanding." I turned slightly, the better to view Royal's profile. "What's he doing with it? Running fingerprints or something?"

Royal nodded. "Maybe. I'll bet Deputy Sterling checked with your friend to see if her ring was missing and if so, when it went missing."

"I never thought about that," I conceded. "I should have called Sporty and asked her."

"Let him handle it. Believe me, when you're a cop, the last thing you want is a civilian butting in and messing up a case."

"Butting in? Making a phone call? I should have called her anyway, to see how she's doing. They had a break-in at their house."

"Really? When?"

I told him what Vaughan told me. By the time I finished, we were entering the parking lot for the restaurant. "Well, that explains why your friend was anxious to take possession of that ring," Royal said. "It might be tied to that robbery. If so, he'll want to make sure to work with the police in Florida."

That made sense, I decided, falling in to step with Royal to go into the building. "I never considered that angle."

"If you're a cop, you think that way." Royal gave his name to the maître d' who protected the entrance to the dining room. We left our coats at the coat-check desk and followed the officious little man into the main dining room.

It was a spectacular setting and would be even more amazing in the summertime, when daylight held on so much longer. Now dusk was settling in and the far edges of the reservoir, a mile or more away, were just faint outlines. The lights of houses dotting the shore were like jewels hanging in the distance.

Our table was at a window above the water below. We ordered drinks while studying the menu, then ordered our meals and sat back. "Here's to new friendships." Royal raised his drink.

I clicked my Moscow Mule mug against his martini glass. "I have a confession to make," I said with a sheepish smile. "Vaughan is the one who got my profile set up and who matched us. Ever since he and Finn got married, he's been trying to find me a special someone."

"Really? I'm flattered that he thinks I'm special." Royal's bemused smile made his green eyes twinkle with mischief.

"Well, it's not just that," I admitted. "You see, whenever my friends and I get together, Sporty and Nimble—my friends from Florida—they always sort of lord it over me that they have each other and they have this perfect married life together. Vaughan thought it wouldn't hurt if I had a date to show them that the single life can be pretty perfect, too."

Royal's smile widened. "You mean I'm the arm candy for you to parade in front of your friends? Now I *am* flattered." He sipped his drink, chuckling. "They must be special friends to still come with all that's going on, what with the robbery and all."

"Like I said, we've been through a lot together.

Now that we're getting older, I think we all feel the need to make sure we stay in touch. But I can appreciate how spooked they must have been with that break-in. I felt that way last night."

"Really? Why? Did something happen?" Gone was the laid-back, relaxed guy. Royal's gaze sharpened and focused on me. I had the feeling the cop-guy was here, not the charming-guy.

"No, nothing really happened. I suppose I was just nervous because of that car that almost ran into me." I sipped my Mule, savoring the tart flavor.

"What? You didn't say you had an accident. When did that happen?"

"An almost-accident," I corrected. "When I was driving home last night. I got to the hill in front of my house. This car came out of nowhere, bright lights on and driving way too fast for a slippery country street. I'm lucky I didn't go into the ditch." I stared at the mesmerizing scenery outside the window, the dark water and lights in the distance hypnotic.

"You didn't mention that last night when I called." His voice was mild, but I thought I heard an undercurrent of concern or maybe criticism.

That was stupid. Why would he care? "I guess I was discombobulated about the light being on in my shop. When I got home, I saw a light on out there and the door was unlocked."

He paused, his drink raised halfway to his lips. "What?" He slowly lowered the glass, his eyes fixed on me.

"Yeah, I could have sworn I locked it up the other day, but I guess I didn't. And now I find that ring in there. I told Finn all about it."

Royal nodded thoughtfully. "Good that you did. It's important to track that kind of thing."

"What kind of thing?"

He sort of shook himself. "Nothing."

"I've been distracted lately," I confessed. "The sale of the shop sort of threw me for a loop. My father and I argued about selling that parcel of land. I was overruled by him and my stepmother."

Royal gave me that half-twitch smile of his. "I still find it hard to think of her as your stepmother."

"No kidding," I muttered. "She's twenty years younger than me and has all the motherly instincts of a feral cat. Of course, my father didn't marry her for her generous disposition." I was surprised to see his expression of distaste or maybe disagreement. "What? Do you think she's America's sweetheart?"

He shrugged. "I just met her briefly, so I can't say. But, well, maybe your father loves her."

I gave him my best *who are you kidding?* look. "I'm sure he loves certain parts of her," I snapped.

"All I'm saying is maybe he was lonely. From what you told me, your mother died a long time ago and he spent most of his life raising you. Then you went off to college. Suddenly you were a grown-up and he was alone. Maybe there was a void in his life that needed to be filled."

I knew what kind of void he wanted to fill, but I kept my mouth shut about *that*. "We had a good life," I said. "At least, we did until she came along."

Royal gently twirled the gin in his glass before taking a sip. "It's a heady experience for a man when a beautiful woman takes an interest in him. I can understand his emotions. I'm at that age where I'm starting to wonder if, well, if I'm washed up and on the shelf." His deep green eyes met mine with frank curiosity. "If a beautiful woman were to tell me that she found me attractive—that would certainly make me sit up and take notice."

I wasn't willing to let my father off the hook so easily. "Especially if she's young and sexy."

Royal reached across the table and took my hand. "Or mature and sexy," he murmured. "As far as I'm concerned, it's the woman, not her age, that matters."

I saw something intriguing in his green eyes.

Chapter 5

Our food, luckily, came soon after that. I say "luckily" because I was starting to get hot and bothered. Who knows what we might have done if we weren't distracted. I barely remembered what I ate—a pork chop, maybe? With a potato? Whatever it was, it tasted like ambrosia. Or maybe it was just the company I was keeping.

We were sipping a cup of coffee after the meal when my phone, somewhere in the depths of my purse, chimed "Family Tradition" by Hank Williams, Jr., my ringtone for my father. "I'm sorry." I picked up my purse and stood. "I should answer this in case—" I shrugged. "In case."

Royal nodded. "Of course." He stood when I left the table, heading for the lobby.

I pulled the phone out. "Hey, Roy." I sank down onto a settee near the front door.

"Where have you been?" he demanded breathlessly. "I've called your house for the past hour. You know I don't like calling your mobile phone."

I frowned. "I didn't know that. I'm out to dinner with a friend. I've been gone for the last hour or two and haven't been home."

"I need to see you right away. Come to the house. And bring your copy of my will. I need to check something. I think she changed it."

"I can't come to see you. Like I said, I'm out to dinner." I peeked at the dining room. I had no idea where this night was headed but I was willing to find out.

Any romantic ideas I had was squashed, though, at Roy's next words. "Don't you understand? She's doing something to disinherit you. We have to make sure she doesn't succeed." He sounded panicked, tearful. I could imagine him clinging to the phone, his plain face distraught.

"There isn't any way she can do that," I said soothingly. "Only a lawyer can change your will. She can't do a damn thing to—"

"Please, Natalie. I have to see you. I need to make sure my copy is correct. Please."

I sighed. When Roy called me *Natalie*, I knew it was serious. "I'm not sure how soon I can get there," I said. "Can't this wait until morning?"

"My God, don't you understand? Don't you care about me? I thought you loved me. I need your help and I don't need it tomorrow, I need it now. There's no telling what she'll do. She's taken the car keys and she won't let me drive. I'm a prisoner here."

Guilt and worry nudged me. I remembered Paul's comment about Aurora showing up with Roy at an appointment. She wasn't keeping a rein on him, was she? "You know I love you. It's just that—" *I'm on a date with a sexy guy and I'd love to see what he has in mind.* I sighed again.

"I need to check this. I'm counting on you. You need to get here in the next half-hour. She's left the house. If you bring your copy of the will, I can compare them before she gets back. She's at a meeting. She goes every Wednesday night." Roy laughed harshly. "It's like AA or something."

AA? Alcoholics Anonymous? Aurora was an alcoholic? I tried to recall what I'd seen of her and drinking, but nothing stood out. If she were an alcoholic, though, that might account for some of the mood swings I'd seen her exhibit and the way she was treating Roy.

"I'll get there as soon as I can." I stood. "But I don't know if I can get there in a half-hour."

"Try, honey. Please." He hung up.

I tucked the phone back in my purse and went into the dining room. Royal tapped the bill folder sitting on the table. "If there's a problem, we can leave right now. I already settled our tab."

"Thank you," I said as he stood. "I'm sorry, but tonight I'm the one who has to cut things short. My father is upset about something, and I need to go to see him."

"Can I drive you?" Royal fell into step with me. "Where's he live?"

"I need to stop at my house first." I had an unofficial copy of Roy's will, one that he had insisted I keep when he and Aurora got married. It was stashed in a fireproof box in my closet.

"I'd be happy to go with you," Royal said as he retrieved our coats, holding mine for me.

I thought about it while we suited up. Roy was northwest of where we were now. My house was slightly north but mostly west. It would save time if Royal drove me to my house then to Roy's. And, I admitted in the secret places of my mind, that meant I'd have him with me when I dealt with Roy and, possibly, with Aurora. Her radar yesterday when she saw Royal told me that he might be just the diversion I needed.

"It would be nice if you could drive," I said while we walked out to the parking lot. The night was clear and cold, with fragments of snow still on the grass and lining the curbs. "My house is mostly west of here. We can swing by there, get what I need, then go to Roy's house. Then you can take me back to my truck and I'll drive home from there."

Royal opened the door for me on his SUV. "Just point me in the right direction."

I smiled at the image that conjured up. I wasn't a person to jump into bed with a guy, but I was starting to have thoughts in that direction. I couldn't remember the last time I had such a nice night out. I shelved that idea while I considered a route to get to my house using back roads. Soon we were speeding through the dark, the moon white and bright above us.

"I love driving in the country at night," Royal commented. "It feels like being on another planet. I'm so glad I moved back here."

"Moved back? Where were you before?" I leaned against my door, letting me see his profile while he drove.

"I was out in California for a while. I really hated that. I don't care what anybody says, having nice weather is no compensation for traffic jams and rude people."

I smiled. "I like having the change of seasons. It's a way to count off where you are in the year." I waved at the outside world. "Snow means Christmas and fireplaces and hot chocolate. Crunchy leaves mean football games and runs to the antique store. Tulips and daffodils mean it's time to start gardening. And hot weather means early days on the golf course then being a slug by the swimming pool in the afternoon."

He chuckled. "You have it all mapped out."

"You bet. I've lived here all my life. I know how to maximize the seasons. How long since you moved back?"

"Like I said, I was in California for a time then I was transferred to Chicago. I've been in the Midwest for about six years." He glanced at me. "I think I'll retire here."

"Not many people would think about retiring in Forestville, Iowa," I said teasingly. "It's not exactly the hub of excitement."

"I can always travel if I want to find excitement. No, this place suits me. I like the people here." He extended his right hand and I put mine in his. He squeezed my fingers gently, then he raised my hand and kissed it before putting it back on the seat, his hand covering mine.

It was surprisingly comfortable and erotic at the same time. We drove in silence, with me giving him the turns as needed. It wasn't until we were almost to my house that I realized I felt safe with him. I hadn't considered the implications of having him come to my home, being there with me alone. It felt like the most natural thing in the world for him to be with me.

"Is this where it happened? Where that car surprised you?" Royal asked when he slowed to make the turn into my lane.

"Yep. I was slowing down, just like you're doing, and he came out of nowhere. Although now that I think about it, maybe he came out of there." I pointed to a break in the trees on the right side of the street, about twenty yards ahead of us. It was part of a snowmobile path leading to the longer snowmobile trail that wound through our neighborhood. The beaten-down ground was barely wide enough for a car, but it was certainly long enough for a car to back in and not be seen from the road.

Royal drove slowly past the spot, then turned around in Doc Small's driveway and came back, pulling over to stare at the declivity. "It does appear that somebody's been in there recently. There's some mud all churned up."

"There's not enough snow yet for a snowmobiler, so that must have been where he was. I'll bet it was somebody who was turning around. I probably startled him when I came over the hill." I nodded, imagining the scenario. "Yeah, that makes sense."

Royal turned into my lane, which was mostly cleared of snow from a combination of sunlight and cars driving on it. There was still snow on the leafy and grassy areas, though, all of it crisscrossed with deer tracks and other critters prints, making irregular patterns. I directed Royal to park in the driveway at the house, the motion light coming on and illuminating the area.

When I got out of the SUV, I noticed the snow in front of my workshop. It had been undisturbed this morning, but now I saw tracks there.

Foot tracks, not critter tracks.

I stared at them, trying to remember — did Vaughan or Finn walk over to the side? I could tell where their vehicle had parked. The tire tracks were still visible in the clotted clumps of snow.

Royal came around the SUV and joined me. "Is that your shop? The one with the light on that was unlocked last night?"

I nodded. "I don't remember seeing footprints when I left tonight." I pointed to the tracks in the snow.

"Why don't I check?" He didn't give me a chance to say 'yea' or 'nay', but instead he went down the slippery steps that connected the house driveway with the shop driveway. I started to follow, but he turned and held up a hand. "Let me check it out." He unbuttoned his overcoat, pushing it back. I realized he had his hand on the butt of the gun in the holster on his waist.

"Sholey hits," I breathed. Once again, I had that sense of two men in front of me: the laid-back, charming guy was now the on-point cop, accustomed to danger and—

And what? I had no idea. I made a mental note to talk to Vaughan about this. I had the feeling there were things I needed to know if I was going to stick with Royal. As I watched him prowl around the outside of my shop, testing the door and going to the side, I knew that there wasn't any question about that. I wanted to know more about this man.

I wanted to know *a lot* more.

Royal returned, pulling his coat closed, which I took to mean there was no longer any threat. He paused, examining the mucked-up snow where Vaughan's SUV sat earlier that day. Then he came back up the steps to where I stood watching. "Somebody parked there and then walked around the building." He pointed to the area in front of the shop.

"Finn and Vaughan were here today. Remember?" I led the way to the garage's side door, opening it with the keys I fished out of my purse.

"There are two different sets of tire marks." He followed me inside, waiting until I flicked on the interior light.

"How do you know there are two sets?" I crossed the garage to the steps leading into the house. One kind of tire looked pretty much the same to me.

"It's a cop thing. Why don't you let me go inside first? Can I have the keys?"

"I don't lock that door." I shrugged when he shot me a disbelieving look. "I know, I know. I'm too trusting. Everybody tells me that. I keep the garage door locked. I guess I never got in the habit of locking the house door."

"You should get in the habit." He went ahead of me, opening the door and going inside without waiting for me. I started to protest this ungentlemanly behavior, then I realized he was acting like a cop again.

Mr. Gold, alert to an alien male presence, wandered into the kitchen, mewing plaintively. Royal eyed the enormous cat. "That's an impressively sized animal." He lowered his hand cautiously, and Mr. Gold gave it a thorough sniff.

"He's a beast, all right," I agreed.

Royal straightened. "Well, your cat isn't skittish, so things are probably okay."

"Come on, I'll give you the tour." I moved past him into the kitchen, gesturing. "Kitchen, living room," I moved into the adjoining room. "Bathroom, den," I said, walking down the hallway. I came to my bedroom and opened the closet door. "I need to get something here." I knelt, opening the small safe.

Royal stood behind me, surveying my closet. His

head tilted to one side when he saw my clothes aligned there. "Wait a minute—you only wear black, white, and gray?" He eyed my sparse wardrobe. "And red," he amended.

"Yep." I peered over my shoulder at him from where I crouched. "I have bib overalls and a couple of pairs of jeans, too, but those are for yard work and shop work."

"Are you color blind?"

"No, just lazy. If you limit your choices, it makes it easy to decide."

"Interesting philosophy."

"It suits me. I don't care about style so why should I waste time trying to match clothes?" I straightened, holding the file containing Roy's legal papers. "Plus it saves a lot of time."

"I imagine it does." He nodded to the folder. "Is that what you needed?"

"Yep. Let's head out to Dad's house."

"If you don't mind, I'd like to check the rest of your house." He gave me that half-smile when I shot him an incredulous look. "Once a cop, always a cop. I won't rest easy tonight unless I'm sure you're safe." He stepped closer to me. "Now one way to keep you safe would be to keep you with me, but maybe that's rushing things a bit."

I was suddenly breathless. "I guess that depends on how close you want to keep me," I murmured.

His arms went around me. "Right now, I think it's pretty darn close." He lowered his head, and our lips met.

We were both tentative at first. It had been a long time since I had a man in my arms and he was so tall and, well, there was just so much of him. But within seconds our kiss deepened, and I forgot all about height differences. I felt like a kid again, newly awakened to passion. I wrapped my arms around his neck and lost myself in the sensation, gripping the folder with one hand and standing on my tiptoes to reach his face.

When we separated, his hands were on my waist, pulling me against his body. I stared into his eyes which seemed to have become an even darker green. "I usually don't move this fast with a lady," he said, his voice husky.

I reluctantly released him, stepping back. As I did, his coat shifted. I saw the gun, nestled into a holster at his waist. "We've got all the time in the world," I said. "I'm willing to take it slow if you are."

Royal put his hand against my face then he gently kissed me, our lips barely brushing. "Going slow sounds good. I'm yours to command."

Now *that* was a heady proposition. "Right now, I need to deal with my father." I held up the folder, which was a bit crinkled from my grip. "Let's take care of that. Then we'll see what the night might bring."

"I like the way you think." Royal followed me back to the kitchen.

"The basement is down that way." I gestured to the stairs leading downward. Miss Copper glared up at us from the small landing at the foot of the stairs. "That's my other cat. She's not much good with strangers. I'm surprised she came out of hiding."

Royal started down the steps. "I told you, I won't rest easy until I've checked everything out. Come on. Continue the tour."

Miss Copper saw us heading her way and raced

into the laundry room. I obligingly showed Royal around the basement, and he opened every door, checked every lock and every window. When we left the house, he waited until I locked the kitchen door behind me. "Get in that habit," he said.

"Will do," I lied. We drove out of my neighborhood, and I gave Royal directions to Roy's house. Ten minutes later we pulled into the driveway. The garage door was closed but Roy's truck still sat in the drive, apparently unmoved since I was there earlier in the day.

We went to the front door, where I rang the bell. It took Roy a few minutes to answer. When he did, he seemed surprised to see us, or maybe he was just surprised to see me with Royal. I was relieved to see he had changed his clothes and now wore jeans and a V-neck navy sweater over a T-shirt.

"I'm sorry to interrupt your evening." He threw open the door and gestured us inside. "Maybe I'm just being foolish, but I thought it was important or I wouldn't have called."

"It's okay. Brendan and I were just finishing up dinner. Brendan, this is my dad, Roy DeWitt. Roy, this is Brendan Royal."

They shook hands then Dad led the way into his former office. "Maybe there's nothing to worry about but you know how you get an idea in your head and you just can't let it go?"

"I know how that is," Royal said. "It'll just bug you until you deal with it." He smiled at me.

"Once a cop, always a cop," I muttered.

"What?" Roy asked.

"Nothing." I handed him the folder. "This is the

copy you gave me a few years ago. I don't know if it was changed since then."

Roy took the folder and went to the love seat farthest away from the doorway. "Please, sit down." He gestured to the other love seat.

We took a seat. I watched Roy while he examined the legal papers in the folder. He appeared to be calm, even unconcerned. This was a complete turnaround from the way he sounded on the phone. He also seemed better than he had that morning. His cheeks were flushed, his shoulders were straight and upright. He was strong and solid. This was the father I remembered. I must have caught him at a bad time that morning, I decided.

Royal's gaze took in the white inset bookcases with the books all aligned, a few photographs here and there. "This is a charming room," he said. "Very restful and nice."

Roy nodded. "Aurora chose the furniture and the paint colors," he said. "I like it." He returned his gaze to the papers on his lap, angling a page to the floor lamp near his shoulder.

I remembered the room as it used to be. Roy's desk was always stacked with journals and books interspersed with business papers and receipts. In the corner where the piano now sat was his drawing table, tilted to catch the best light from the window on his latest landscape design. A couple of mismatched armchairs completed the furniture in the room with the bookcases serving as a storage place for more magazines and books, haphazardly arranged.

This pretty, serene room full of soft chairs and gentle pictures was a far cry from that active workman's space. I started to say something to that effect, but at that moment headlights shone into the room. "That must be Aurora." Roy stood, smiling. "She has a meeting she goes to every Wednesday." He left the folder on the love seat and went out of the room, heading for the kitchen, which had an entry door to the garage.

"That's odd," I said, getting up. "Roy was so anxious to review these papers before Aurora came home. Now he acts like it doesn't matter at all."

"Maybe he just doesn't want to upset her," Royal said.

"That's not how he sounded on the phone." I shook my head. "Something just isn't adding up."

We heard voices in the hall leading to the kitchen, then Aurora came into the room, still wearing her red winter coat. "Two visits in one day." She smiled coolly at me. "What a surprise." Her flat tone of voice told me what she thought of the 'surprise.' Her gaze shifted to Royal. "Hello again. Mr. Royal, wasn't it?" She began to shrug out of her coat.

Royal stepped forward and held the coat for her. "You've got a good memory," he said. "I hope you don't mind us dropping by."

"Of course not." Aurora's voice was just barely polite. She took the coat from Royal and went to the hall closet.

"I asked Snow to come over when she had the chance," Roy said, coming back into the room. "I wanted to check on something about the sale papers. I couldn't put my hands on it. I'm not sure where I put it."

"Couldn't it wait until tomorrow?" Aurora

snapped. She must have realized how shrewish she sounded because she smiled tiredly. "I'm sorry. I have a bit of a headache, and I had a difficult meeting tonight."

Now that she mentioned it, she did appear haggard. There was a pinched look around her eyes. Maybe it was a lack of makeup, I decided. I usually saw her all prettied up, but tonight she was almost like a normal person with her hair pulled untidily back, a simple striped sweater and dark blue pants. "I can make a copy of what you want and drop it off tomorrow," I suggested.

"I can make a copy," Aurora said. "I have a printer that's a copier in my office. Which paper is it?"

I thought I saw panic in Roy's dark eyes. I went to the love seat and picked up the folder. "It was this one, wasn't it?" I shuffled through the pages, finding a copy of the final inventory from my store. "I haven't updated it, though. Why don't I do that? Then I'll make sure you get a copy." I tucked it back into the folder and jammed the folder under my arm. "I sold a few things earlier this week, so I need to note those on the list."

"That's fine," Roy said. "Yes, that makes sense. We need a complete list, don't we?" He started toward the door, and we fell in with him, Aurora trailing behind us. "If you can update it then make a copy for me, that would be perfect."

"I'll handle it," I promised. I kissed his cheek, and he pulled me to him for a brief hug.

"Thank you, Princess," he whispered. "I love you."

"I love you, too, King Daddy." I saw Aurora watching us, her icy blue eyes emotionless. "I'll drop that off when I can." I smiled perfunctorily at Aurora and went to the door.

Royal opened it for me then turned. "Good night." He nodded to Roy. Then he smiled at Aurora and she visibly softened, her stiff body relaxing. "Good night."

"I'm sorry," I muttered as we walked to his SUV. "I guess we'll deal with it later." When Aurora's not around, I thought but didn't say.

Royal opened the car door for me, peering over the top of the vehicle at the house. "I think it relieved his mind that you came over. I know a nice little bar not too far from here. Why don't we have an after-dinner drink then I'll drive you back to your truck?"

"Thanks. I'd love that." I watched him walk around the SUV to get into the driver's seat. What a guy. Not only did he not complain that our evening was cut short, but he understood how my father felt and, more importantly, my sense of obligation. He slipped into the driver's seat, and I leaned close to him. "Hey," I murmured.

"Hmm?" He leaned toward me.

I tugged on his coat. "Get over here so I can kiss you."

He obliged, and I did just that. When we broke apart a minute later, he smiled at me. "What was that for?"

I leaned back. "Thanks."

"Man, if that's the thanks I get for tagging along with you to visit your family, I wonder what will happen when I really do something for you."

I grinned. "Stick with me and you'll find out."

"Promises, promises."

He drove to a small neighborhood bar called the The Silver Penny, tucked back behind a strip mall. We got a table in the corner and a couple of glasses of wine and sat and talked for an hour. I finally reluctantly said, "I'd better go before I get too relaxed. I still have to drive home from the eastside store."

"You can leave the truck there. I can take you home now then I'll pick you up in the morning to go get your truck."

Or I could invite him in tonight and he could drive me over in the morning. I know he was thinking the same thing from the way he smiled slowly, his eyes intent on me. I studied him, knowing this was an opportunity that I might regret missing.

Then something changed. Royal seemed to somehow recede from me, like he thought of something that made him hesitate. He pulled out his wallet and put a bill on the table. "We'd better get going before we both get so relaxed we can't move. I'll take you to get your truck, but I insist on following you home. I want to make sure you get there okay."

"Thanks. I'd like that."

"And when we get back to your house, I want to see every light come on inside. Then you come out on the front porch and wave to me. That way I'll know it's all okay."

I breathed a sigh of relief. I knew I didn't dare invite him inside, but I also knew that I wanted that sense of safety he gave me. "That's a perfect solution."

He grinned. "It's not perfect, but it's close."

An hour later, I waved good-bye to him while he drove down my drive. I shut off the lights, walking into the living room to stare at the yard outside. The wind was blowing strongly out of the north, the branches of the trees swaying and dipping. I sank down on the couch, thinking about the last kiss we shared, standing in the parking lot at the eastside store. Heavens, I couldn't remember the last time I felt this tingly in certain areas of my body. When I hit menopause, I assumed those kinds of sensations were behind me.

What an odd turn of circumstance if the best years might really be ahead of me. I leaned on the back of the couch, staring at the yard outside, illuminated by the yard light and feeble moonglow.

That's when I saw the footprints in the snow near the tree line.

Chapter 6

I picked up my mobile phone, my first thought being *Call Royal.* I tapped my *Contacts* icon and my finger hovered over his name.

Wait a minute. I stood, peering out the window. Did Royal go around behind my shop earlier? Maybe those were his footprints. I hadn't looked out this window when we were in the house, did I?

I sat back down, my mind whirling. If I called Royal and asked him, I'd have an answer. If they were his footprints then I would seem like a nervous Nelly. What if he said no, he didn't walk around the yard? Either way, he'd probably come over to either calm a nervous Nelly or—

Or what? What could he do? Well, I knew what he and I *could* do. I was almost sure his earlier reluctance was only temporary. It was probably a result of him taking a mental step back and thinking, hey, we're rushing into something.

Something. But what? I barely knew the guy. Sure, it felt like he had been a part of my life for years, but really, what did I know about him? Did I want a man in my life? Because I was sure of one thing—if I fell into bed with Brendan Royal, he was going to become a part of my life. I just had that feeling with him. He wasn't a love-'em-and-leave-'em kind of guy. No, Royal was solid and sweet and, well, permanent. I could easily imagine a life with him.

I stared at the back yard. Was there any danger? No, there wasn't. The prints didn't come up to the house. They were at the perimeter, out near the tree line by the shop. It was probably Royal who made them. Besides, all the doors and windows were locked, and I had Finn and 911 on speed dial.

No, I'd been taking care of myself for more than thirty years. I might decide to let Royal into my life at some point. I sure as hell wasn't going to start out anything serious with him based on a nameless fear on my part. There was no way he was going to see me as a helpless female needing his assistance.

Reassured by my internal pep talk, I went to bed, Miss Copper taking her accustomed spot next to my feet and Mr. Gold settling in at the window. *My guard cats,* I thought then I drifted off to sleep.

I spent Thursday morning puttering in my workshop, taking my time to clean my golf clubs and inspect the grip on each club. When I ran the store, I barely had a moment to wipe down the clubs and clean out my bag because I was always getting ready for the holidays coming up. Now I had the luxury of time. At first, I was worried about how I would occupy my days. But it was late morning before I checked the clock. I realized I needed to change out of my work clothes and get going to meet the first of the weekend arrivals.

This retirement stuff was a blessing and a curse, I decided while I pulled on a red sweatshirt decorated with dancing snowmen. I pulled my hair back with a red and white headband, tugged on black jeans, and was out the door, on my way to the bar downtown where I was to meet Nerdy and Vaughan for lunch.

Yes, retirement was a curse in the sense that it made me realize time was slipping away. I would be fifty-six in two months. What did I have to show for my life? Most people had accomplishments, children, careers. What could I realistically hope to do in my remaining thirty years, God willing?

On the other hand, retirement offered unlimited possibilities. I was luckier than most with my nest egg and so little debt. I could travel, I could spend time learning new things, I could take classes or get a part-time job or investigate new hobbies. I was active and had few health issues except for the occasional ache and pain. I had years ahead of me for whatever might strike my fancy.

Perhaps that was the odd part about it. For so long I had been focused on the business, making a go of the shop, working with my father to keep the landscape and nursery a success. What did strike my fancy? My interests had always centered around what would be useful for our business. Now that wasn't a concern.

Who was I when I wasn't thinking about the store?

I parked in a downtown lot and hurried along windswept streets to the corner bar, not far from the Interstate bisecting the city. This little hole-in-the-wall spot had been our regular gathering place since we started these reunion weekends. On the Thursday of the weekend, whoever was in town would go to the bar, and we'd spend two or three hours together before people left to spend the rest of the day with their families. On Friday evening, we would take in a game of whatever sport was in season. On Saturday afternoon, everyone came to my house for barbeque, regardless of the weather. The out-of-towners dispersed on Sunday to all corners of the United States, leaving me, Vaughan, and Finn—the homebodies—behind.

I entered the bar, pausing to let my eyes get accustomed to the gloom. It was a shabby but cozy little place. It had been there for decades, the ownership passing from parent to child and then child again. I spied Nerdy in a booth opposite the long, oval-shaped bar. I made my way through the lunchtime crowd and leaned over to kiss him.

"Oh, Snow, you never change," he said with a grin when I slipped into the seat opposite him. "You're still the most beautiful girl in the room."

I slid my jacket off and regarded him across the scarred table. Iven "Nerdy" Maly was the epitome of *plain*, with his chubby face, equally chubby body, thinning blond hair pulled back in a queue hanging down his back, and his sparse little goatee clinging to his chin. He could pass unnoticed in any crowd, just another middle-aged couch potato who probably drove a minivan and cheered his football team on from the depths of his recliner.

Little would anyone know that he had contributed to one of the biggest tech giants in the country, that he retired at the age of forty-five to an estate in southern California, and he was still sought after at conferences highlighting the hippest computer games. Nerdy was probably the smartest guy I knew, and one of the sweetest. He was married and divorced and now living with a girl half his age who doted on him, or so it seemed. I'm sure his fortune helped her affection, but I think she honestly cared for him. Besides, who was I to criticize a person's romantic choices?

That made me think of my father and Aurora. I

suddenly remembered Roy's odd behavior the night before. I needed to make a copy of the legal papers and get them to him without Aurora being any the wiser. That would take some planning on my part. I shoved that worry to one side for the moment.

"It's good to see you, Nerdy. How was your flight? Uneventful? Did you change planes in Denver?"

He nodded. "It's a pain in the butt to get here, but at least the weather cooperated. Yeah, I flew from LAX to Denver, then Denver to here. No major snowstorms, no ice storms, and all flights were on time." He regarded me with a lopsided smile. "It seems like whenever we get together, we're always blessed with good weather. I think you're our good luck charm, Snow."

I plucked a laminated menu from the holder at the side of the table. "Maybe Hopeful or Calm are the charms, not me," I said. "They live in town, too."

"But you were always the one who made things go smoothly. You were the one we went to when we had problems. Heck, you're still the first person I think of to call when I'm not sure what to do. I'll bet Sporty and Nimble call you, too. I know Brainy and Bitchy used to call you. They'd talk to you then call me."

"I dispense advice now and then," I conceded. "It's probably good for you guys to get an outside opinion sometimes."

"It's good to get your opinion," he corrected. "I don't know how you do it. Any time I'm not sure about what to do, I give you a call or drop you an email. We hash through it, and somehow a solution appears." He sipped his beer. "You're magical that way."

I had more common sense than most of them, but I

didn't voice that opinion. "You haven't needed any advice from me for a long time, so I guess that means things are going good."

As I hoped, he launched into a recap of the past year, telling me about his travels and the remodeling he and his girlfriend were doing at the ranch he bought. Nerdy was just finishing a story about a fiasco with the hot tub when I spied Vaughan coming into the bar. I waved him over, and he dropped into the booth next to me.

"Hey, Nerdy, good to see you." he said, peeling off his gloves. "You guys won't believe this. I just heard from Sporty's daughter. They had a car accident on the way to the airport."

"What? Today? Weren't they flying out this morning?" I turned to Nerdy. He nodded in confirmation.

"Sporty gave her daughter my phone number for this weekend. You know, just some contact information in case it was needed. Apparently, Sporty and Nimble were driving to the airport. Somebody ran a red light and plowed into them where they were coming through the intersection. The guy who hit them ran away. Literally. I mean, he just abandoned the car and ran." Vaughan shook his head at this evidence of asshole-ness. "Can you believe it?"

"That's crazy." Nerdy pushed a menu across the table to Vaughan. "The jerk probably didn't have insurance so he was scared about a lawsuit or something. That kind of shit happens all the time in L.A."

"Are they okay? Were they hurt?"

"Her daughter just said they were in the emergency

room. She was with them. She sounded really shook up."

"No wonder. That's horrible." I smiled apologetically at the waitress, who appeared at the table, a pitcher of beer and three glasses on her tray. "Sorry, we've barely checked the menu."

"No hurry. Here you go." She set down the beer. "I'll be back to get your order in a minute. Take your time."

Nerdy filled the three glasses, and we all raised them. "To absent friends." I clicked mine against theirs. We all took a swallow and lowered our glasses. "We'll have to find out what hospital they're in." I picked up the menu again. "Send them flowers."

"Finn is already on it," Vaughan said.

"Finn? Why?"

Vaughan studied his menu. "The call came in while Finn was standing there. You know how he is, he's got to get the details about everything. I think I'll get the hot roast beef. They do it good here."

Nerdy laughed. "What's to do good? It's a slab of Iowa beef, potatoes, and gravy."

"The gravy makes all the difference," Vaughan pointed out.

"Speaking of which, how's the business?"

Vaughan began a summary of his year, but I only half-listened. Poor Sporty and Nimble. I was in the hospital once when I broke my arm twenty years ago. I had only vague memories of it, but I remember it being noisy and worrisome. If they were T-boned like that, it's likely somebody had at least one or two broken bones. God knows what happened to them with the airbags going off.

"…retired now, right, Snow?"

I turned my attention back to my companions. "Say what?"

"I said, now you're retired, too," Vaughan said. "Life of leisure and all that. Plus she's got a hot boyfriend." He winked at Nerdy.

"It's about damn time." Nerdy raised his beer. "I wish Sporty was here. She'd be even more green with envy than she usually is."

The waitress walked over, her notepad out. "Made up your mind on lunch?"

We all placed our orders then I asked, "What's that mean? Sporty isn't envious of me."

Vaughan almost choked on his beer. "You are so clueless, Snow."

"Enlighten me, please," I snapped. "What's there to be envious about? She's the one who has the perfect family and the perfect husband and the perfect life." My gaze shifted from Nerdy to Vaughan, who shook his head. "You and I were just talking about this the other day, how she likes to lord it over me that she's so happy."

"Yeah, well, it was all bullshit," he muttered.

"She and Nimble were talking about divorce," Nerdy said.

"What? You're kidding. They've been married forever." I nudged Vaughan, and he grunted painfully. "Why didn't you tell me about this?"

"I wasn't sure. Nimble mentioned they were having problems last year. I thought maybe they'd patched it up." He sipped his beer, glancing sideways at me. "Look at it from her point of view. Here you are, pretty and sexy and single."

I snorted derisively. "One out of three ain't bad."

"There she is," he barreled ahead, "married to a guy who's had affairs since day one, the kids all gone, no career to fall back on, and facing unmarried life while her husband is cavorting with a younger woman."

"Oh, no," I murmured. "He didn't?"

"He did," Nerdy said with a sad shake of his head.

"Oh, Sporty." I felt a pang of sympathy for my old friend. "I wish I'd known."

"She didn't want anybody to know," Nerdy said. "I mean, all these years she's been talking up her perfect life and now—poof." He gestured expressively. "All gone."

"Maybe this accident will bring them back together," Vaughan said. "There's nothing like shared adversity to make people remember why they fell in love in the first place."

I rested my head briefly on his shoulder. "And that's how you got the nickname of Hopeful."

"I guess you can see why she envied you," Nerdy said. "You always succeeded at anything you tried. Great golfer, successful in business, happy in life."

I considered that while we ate our lunch and continued catching up on each other's lives. I suppose it did appear that I had led a charmed life. I graduated from college, went into business with my father, had a few happy love affairs, and was now settling down into my later years with a comfortable retirement and few worries.

It was quite a contrast to the others of our band of merry athletes. It had taken Vaughan and Finn many years before they could settle down together, legally. Bitchy—Charlene—had been thrice divorced. Brainy—

Heidi—had several disastrous love affairs, one of which resulted in a lawsuit that almost bankrupted her. It cost Nerdy a lot of money to get rid of his wife, but maybe he was happy now. And Nimble and Sporty, the supposedly perfect couple, living a lie all these years. When I thought of it that way, then yes, I had indeed lived a charmed life.

The waitress brought our bills and I said to Nerdy, "Tell me what I owe you for the beer."

"Owe me? I thought you bought it."

I shook my head. "Nope, I assumed you did." I looked up at the waitress. "Which tab has the beer? I want to make sure to pay my part."

She jerked a thumb over one shoulder. "The guy at the bar bought it."

"Who?" I half-stood to see if I knew anyone there.

"Who?" Vaughan peered over the crowd. "Which one?"

The waitress turned, scanning the people sitting there. Every barstool was taken with lunchtime diners. "There. At the end of the bar."

I craned my neck, twisting to peek around two men who chose that moment to walk in front of our booth. A man sat at the far end of the bar, near the exit. He raised his hand when he saw me. He was almost familiar, like someone I knew but I wasn't sure where from, a person seen out of context.

Out of context. That was it. He was the guy from the bar when Royal and I went to hear the band. He had taken Royal's seat for a minute and talked to me.

"Let me out," I said to Vaughan, pushing into him with my hip.

"Hold on, give me a minute." Vaughan picked up

his coat and slid out of the booth.

I started toward the bar, but the guy dropped off the barstool and was out the door before I took two steps. "Weird," I muttered. I picked up my tab from the table then walked with my friends to the front of the bar where the checkout line was forming.

"Who was that guy?" Vaughan asked. "The beer buyer?"

"I don't know. I saw him the other night when Royal and I went to the Apple."

"Royal? You're not on a first-name basis with him?"

I shrugged. "I just think of him as Royal, not as Brendan."

"Royalty? You're dating a prince?" Nerdy grinned at me over his shoulder while the waitress handled his bill.

"Prince Charming," Vaughan said. "Mr. Right."

"Mr. Right Now." I handed my tab to the waitress with a twenty, but she waved it away.

"Already paid for." She handed me a receipt and held out her hand to Vaughan, who was next in line.

"Ooh, Snow has a secret admirer," Vaughan said.

"Shut up, Hopeful." I slapped him on the arm. "It's just somebody who knows me from the shop, that's all."

We left the bar, pausing outside on the sidewalk. "Where are we meeting tomorrow night?" Nerdy asked.

"We have tickets to the high school football playoffs." Vaughan tugged his coat collar up against the west wind blowing in off the river. "The Forestville Foxes versus the Woodvale Wolves. A good old showdown between two predators."

I turned to my left and saw a group of older men leaving the restaurant next door. I recognized several of the men. "Hey, I need to talk to somebody. That must be the Kiwanis guys. They have lunch downtown on Thursday." I hugged Nerdy then Vaughan. "I'll meet you guys at the Woodvale stadium tomorrow night."

"Bring your prince," Nerdy said. "And if you get any information about Sporty and Nimble, give me a call. We need to send flowers or something."

"I'll handle it," Vaughan said. He gave me a little shove. "I'll check in with you later."

"Sounds good." I hurried after three of the restaurant attendees, struggling to put names to faces. As I approached, one of the men turned. I vaguely recognized him as someone who used to do business with Roy. I always thought of him as Santa because he had white hair, a white beard, and was rotund and always jolly.

"Natalie, hello! How are you doing?" He held out his hand. "I don't know if you remember me. Bob Cottage. I used to meet your dad now and again for coffee. I had him do some landscaping for us at my office over on the south side of town."

I took his hand. "Of course I remember. How have you been?"

"Fine. We miss seeing your father at our lunches." The other men with him nodded their agreement. "Roy never missed a Kiwanis lunch. He used to say it was his chance to find out the gossip about what was going on in town." Cottage's eyes twinkled.

"Roy was busy with the sale of the westside property," I said. "You know we closed the shop there?"

"Yes, I heard about that. I was sorry to see it go. That's a nice parcel of land. Maybe I'm old-fashioned, but I hate seeing old businesses torn down and these office parks go in their place. But I suppose Roy wasn't up to managing both businesses, what with his health fading and all."

I think I kept my surprise hidden. "I think he felt the strain," I murmured.

"His wife mentioned that it was getting too much for him," Cottage continued. "I have to admit, I wasn't surprised. Those last few landscape projects he worked on just didn't have his usual touch."

"Well, everybody slows down eventually," one of the other men said with a smile. "You know how it goes. A man retires and, before you know it, he's so busy doing other stuff he can't remember to come to lunch."

"That's true," Cottage said. "I mentioned it to Roy the other day. He said he forgot all about it."

"You've seen him lately?" I glanced at the men in turn.

They all nodded. "Sure, we get together, over at that coffee shop by your eastside nursery. Roy used to come by often, but we don't see him much anymore."

"He said he doesn't like to drive," one of the other men said.

"No, he said his wife doesn't like him to drive," another corrected. "I suppose she worries about him after that accident."

I was hard-pressed to keep my face expressionless. "I suppose," I agreed. "Did he tell you about it?"

The man grinned. "He didn't have to tell me about it. I was there. Heck, it's hard not to miss it when somebody mistakes the gas for the brakes and goes over the curb in a parking lot. I'm glad the other guy wasn't hurt."

"Nobody was going very fast," Cottage said. "And it was slippery in that parking lot. I've told that store manager he needs to get a better maintenance crew to handle snow removal." The other man frowned like he wanted to debate that point, but he stayed quiet. "Anyway, it was good seeing you, Natalie. Say hello to your dad the next time you talk."

"I will. Good to see you, too." I watched them walk away then I headed back to my truck. I was almost there when I took a short detour, going two blocks north to stop in at the office of the folks who handled my insurance. I had been meaning to chat with them about changing my policy now that I was no longer at the store. Why not now? And maybe why not find out a little about an accident I knew nothing about?

What else was Aurora hiding from me? Up until three years ago—when he met her—Roy had been in full control of things in his life. He drove to work, he managed two businesses, he made sure payroll got out on time, he paid bills, he handled landscaping projects.

What the hell had she done to him? I crossed the street, checking traffic on my left where the federal courthouse sat at the end of the block. It was an ornate old building that occupied the corner and half of the block behind it. That's when I saw Royal walking down the steps in front of the courthouse. Two women and a man were with him, and they were talking, conferring about something. They stopped at the base of the steps.

I started to wave to him then he pointed at one of the women, obviously angry about something. She returned his glare, turning to the other man as though for support. I decided that maybe I shouldn't interrupt. It might be a business talk of some kind. I continued across the street, pausing outside the insurance office.

The woman not arguing was a striking-looking lady wearing a dark coat, a dark skirt, and high heels, with a large leather bag slung over one shoulder. Attorney, I thought, or executive. She stood next to Royal. I had the impression they were on the same team. Then she turned to him and shook her head, saying something that diverted his ire from the shorter woman. She smiled at him and slapped him playfully on the arm. The man laughed and turned to face me.

I ducked inside. I don't know why, but I didn't want to be seen by Royal at that moment. There was something about the scene that made me uncomfortable. But why? I peeked through the glass on the door to see the small group breaking up. Royal and the attorney were walking away. He had his arm around her shoulders and she was looking up at him with an adoring smile. They disappeared around the corner.

My stomach lurched. Not my business, I told myself fiercely. He's just a guy I know. We have no ties. There's nothing between us.

My stomach still hurt.

Well, there was nothing I could do about it now. I would see Royal that night and I would—

What would I do? Ask him who the woman was with him downtown? It was none of my business, really.

"Can I help you?"

I turned to the receptionist, relieved that I didn't have to think about my dilemma. I was soon ushered back into my agent's office. I explained that I was now semi-retired and should probably review my policy. We chatted about that, then as I was preparing to leave, I said casually, "I wanted to check up on the accident Roy had. You know the one in the parking lot?"

The agent nodded. "Roy was lucky. There were several witnesses, and the other person didn't press charges."

I leaned back in the uncomfortable wooden guest chair. "Press charges? I thought it was just a silly fender bender. At least, that's the way Roy made it sound." I smiled encouragingly.

"I suppose that's how he saw it." The agent frowned, his thin lips almost disappearing with disapproval. "I have to say, I'm glad his wife was there to take care of things."

"I'm sorry. What things?"

"Your father was so upset. It certainly made a poor impression on the police. But she was able to calm him down and smooth things over. He's lucky to have her."

"I'm sure he is," I said slowly.

"We paid all the claims, but it will stay on his record. Although I had the impression the police were recommending that he not drive anymore."

"Isn't that a bit extreme? It's just one little accident."

"That's just it, though. It isn't his only one. It's just the first one involving other people." He stood. "You might want to talk to his wife about it. I'm sure she can fill you in."

I wanted to pump him for more information, but he obviously didn't want to talk. I left soon after that, none the wiser for the conversation. The hell with talking to

Aurora. I needed to talk to Roy and find out what was going on. I glanced to the right, at the courthouse. And I would mention to Royal that I saw him downtown and see what he said. I wasn't going to get involved with anyone if that someone had another person in his life.

Satisfied with that plan of action, I crossed the street and headed to my truck. I pulled out my gloves and the receipt from the bar came with it. I started to wad it up and toss it in the garbage can, but then I spied the fat magic-marker writing on in it. I smoothed it out.

Did you like the ring?

Chapter 7

I took a step back, stumbling on the curb. "What the hell?" I muttered.

I stared down at the crumpled paper. The words were written in all capital letters, red and bright on the receipt.

My first impulse was to throw it away. I felt somehow tainted holding it. Then I realized it might be tied to whatever it was Finn was doing with that ring we found. The sheriff's office was on my way home. I'd stop off and see if Finn were around.

I tucked the receipt in my purse and hurried to my truck. Twenty minutes later I was at the sheriff's department, only to find that Finn wasn't there. I considered leaving the receipt with the guy on duty at the desk, but I had no idea how to explain it to him. So I just left my name and asked that Finn give me a call when he could.

It was only three-thirty but the sun was already getting low in the sky. At this time of year, it seemed like we barely had any daylight. As far as I was concerned, November and February were two of the longest months of the year despite having fewer days. November because it was that ugly in-between month of brown earth and no-snow, and February because by then I was sick of snow and longing for color again.

I drove home, mapping out in my head what I

would say to Royal that night. No matter how I phrased it, I think it sounded accusatory or whiney. I would just have to find the right moment to drop my question into conversation.

When I got to the house, I made sure the shop was securely locked then walked to the back yard. Most of the snow was gone, with just remnants showing in shady spots. Any footprints or tire tracks were gone. I went inside and spent a few minutes on the computer, doing a web search on the musical I'd be seeing that night. I didn't want to be totally clueless. I was glad I did when I read the plot summaries.

Showboat had a long history in the theater and was one of the first so-called 'musical dramas' as opposed to the lightweight musical revues that were prevalent when it first released. I still wasn't sure if I'd like all the singing and dancing as part of the plot, but I had to admit, I was intrigued.

My phone rang, Roy's number on the display. "I was just thinking about calling you," I said when I picked up the receiver.

"You know what they say about great minds," he joked. "I wanted to thank you for driving out to see me last night. I don't know what got in my head. It just seemed so important for me to study my will. I was sure the copy I had here was wrong."

"Do you still want to see my copy?" I asked. "I can make a copy and —"

"No, I talked it over with Aurora, and we went through it all. I'm sure I was just misreading things last night." He gave an unconvincing laugh. "I guess my eyesight must be going or something. And don't worry about that inventory update, either. We've got time to settle all that before tax season next year."

His legal file was still sitting on my desk. "We'll have to start prepping for quarterly estimates, though. So I'll make sure that's updated before we talk to our tax guys." I reached for my desk calendar. "That's the first week of December, isn't it?"

There was a long pause. "Oh, that's right. This is November already. Well, yeah, I guess we will need to start thinking about that. Let's get through Thanksgiving first then we'll work on it. You're coming here, aren't you?"

Roy and I had talked about this a couple of times. "No, I'm spending the day with Finn and Vaughan, remember? Vaughan always cooks up a big meal for the homeless shelter, and I help them dish it out." Ever since Roy and Aurora got married, I spent Thanksgiving and part of Christmas with Vaughan and Finn and their charity work. Better that than sitting and watching my father and his trophy wife act all lovey-dovey.

"Oh, sure, yeah. That's right. I forgot."

"Hey, listen, while you're on the phone. I ran into some of your old cronies today. I was having lunch with Nerdy and Hopeful downtown, and the Kiwanis bunch was lunching."

"I don't see much of them anymore," Roy said. "I guess they decided they're too busy to have coffee. And I just can't get to lunch. It's too much bother to drive all the way downtown just to eat some dried-out sandwiches."

I frowned. This was news to me. Roy used to love his Kiwanis outings. "One of the guys mentioned you had a car accident. What's the deal? What happened?"

There was another long pause. "Oh, it was nothing. It was in the parking lot out at the grocery store, late last spring. We had a hard rain and things froze a bit. The car slid into somebody. You know how that happens."

Well, yeah, I did. You can't live in the Midwest and not have the occasional slip-and-slide in a parking lot. "It sounded like it was bad."

Roy blew out a sigh. "I didn't want to tell anybody about it. You see, Aurora was driving. I told them I was but she was. She's not comfortable driving on snow. I figured it was a good chance for her to get in some practice." He lowered his voice. "Don't tell her that I told you. She's embarrassed about it. She had some other fender-benders. We didn't want this on her record."

I shook my head in confusion. The insurance agent said it was Roy who had the accidents, not Aurora. Surely he would know, right? But if Roy was taking the blame for them maybe he didn't. "No worries," I said.

"Thanks for calling, Princess. It's always good to talk to you. I'd like to get to know your friend better. Maybe you can come out for dinner sometime."

I started to point out that he was the one who called me then I dismissed the thought. "Sure, maybe we can meet someplace."

Roy laughed. "Aurora's not that bad of a cook."

It wasn't her cooking I objected to. It was the way she micro-managed my father's meals, making sure the table was set just so, that the food was arranged a certain way, and that all the courses came out one right after the other. I always felt like I was at a factory or something. "Sure thing, we'll figure out something. I'll talk to you later. If you want a copy of anything, just let me know."

"I will. 'Bye."

I hung up the phone, more confused than ever. Roy said Aurora was driving, and the insurance people said Roy was driving. Who was right? Oh, well. I couldn't answer that one now. I stuck the file back in the safe box and went to the kitchen to feed the critters then fussed with my makeup, something I normally didn't bother much with. But this was a special night, and I wanted to do something special. Then I experimented with my hair, settling on an upswept hair-do held together with bright red combs in strategic locations. I was pleased with the effect contrasted with my gray-and-red top and black pants. A red purse completed my ensemble.

As I was transferring items from one bag to another, I saw the receipt again. I called Vaughan, but my call went straight to his voice mailbox. I wondered how Sporty and Nimble were doing. Maybe he had more news. "Tell Finn to call me when he can," I dictated. "And what did he find out about the accident in Florida? Where do we send flowers? Call me."

I went to my living room window. My house was angled slightly at the top of the hill overlooking a small portion of Apple Lane in the distance. Fingers of setting sunlight stole through the trees, casting long shadows over everything. I thought of my old college classmates, lying in a hospital in Florida. Friendships like ours were rare, I suppose, and that's what made it so precious. I went into my den and stared at the photograph on the wall.

Pretty and laughing Brainy, voted most likely to

become President. Now dead. Bitchy, small and petite but with a golf drive that could outdistance many men. She was dead, too, killed five years ago. There was Nimble with his arm around Sporty. She was tall and blonde, he was tall and dark-haired. They were both tanned and fit and so perfectly matched or so we thought. Vaughan and Finn stood together, Finn with a baseball bat resting on his shoulder, staring straight into the camera with that serious, serene expression of his. And Vaughan was next to him, a tennis racket held in front of him like a shield.

I was in the middle, in front, with all of them grouped around me. My thick white hair was pulled up in a ponytail. I wore my golf shorts and shirt in school colors of pale green and dark green. Good heavens, I was so young and carefree and confident.

Car lights shone outside, and I left the room, picking up my purse before going to the closet for my coat. I felt renewed somehow, as if studying that picture reminded me of what was possible in the world. For so long I had simply gone about the business of living without really thinking about it. But now I had a handsome man waiting to take me out, I had free time ahead of me, and I was beholden to no one for anything.

I smiled, pulling open the door. Carefree, indeed.

"Ready to go?" Royal asked.

I leaned forward and kissed him lightly. "Ready."

He stepped to one side, and I moved past him, pulling the door closed and listening for the click of the lock. "How was your day?" he asked when we walked to his SUV.

"Surprisingly busy." I waited until he was in the

car, then said, "I went downtown for lunch today with one of my friends who's in town for the weekend."

"One of the Seven Jocks?" He put his arm on the back of the seat to peer behind him while he backed up.

"Yep. Nerdy is in town. I met him and Vaughan for lunch. Remember I told you about those friends of ours who had the robbery? They were in a car accident on the way to the airport. I don't think they'll be joining us this weekend."

"In an accident? That's too bad. What happened?"

"I'm not sure. We only got sketchy details. Their daughter called Vaughan. She told him that they were T-boned in an intersection on the way to the airport."

Royal steered us down my winding drive, going slowly while his headlights illuminated the lane. "I'll bet you have a lot of deer," he commented when we came out on Apple Lane.

"More than our share. I don't mind because I don't do a lot of gardening, but some of the neighbors get bent out of shape when their hostas are nibbled." I stared out my window at the lawns sliding past. "The deer and the other critters were here first, so I figure they get dibs on whatever I grow."

"That's a very egalitarian attitude."

"It's the only way to stay sane in suburbia." I turned to regard him. Like me, he wore dark pants, and I spied a green-and-white striped sweater under his dark leather jacket. "Our group always gets together on the Thursday of our weekends for lunch," I said. "While I was downtown, I thought I saw you."

"Around lunchtime?"

"Yep."

"Yeah, I met my little sister downtown. She's a

Federal District Attorney."

I let out a breath I didn't know I was holding. "I saw you guys in front of the courthouse. I had to talk to my insurance people across the street."

"Kim and I sometimes work together," he said, driving to the main road leading to downtown. "I had to meet some people there about a job I'm on. I figured I'd take her out for lunch. But my meeting ran long, and then she had to get to court, so we ended up getting a bagel instead."

"I didn't know you had family in town," I said. "Any other siblings?"

"No, just me and Kim. She lives over by West High, sort of south of you on that side of town. Her husband is an elementary school principal. He used to be with the police department, but it was too tough being married to a D.A."

"Why?"

He glanced at me then returned his attention to the road. I couldn't be sure, but I had the feeling he was gauging my reaction. "The police and the legal people are sometimes on two different sides when it comes to catching criminals."

"But she's a D.A. She's on the cop's side, isn't she?"

He nodded. "But occasionally the police may act in a way that can be awkward when it comes to making a case in a court of law."

I considered that while we merged onto the freeway, joining other traffic going south. "Illegal stuff?" I finally asked.

"Not really. Maybe just…" His hands tightened on the wheel. "Maybe not strictly moral, I guess you could say. Anyway, that was only part of the problem. Her husband was injured on the job. I think that took a toll on their marriage. It's tough to be married to somebody who puts their life on the line. It can be a strain for some people."

"I'm sure it would be. The most stressful thing I ever had to deal with was a customer who insisted on getting their money back for a purchase. Finn mentioned something about that yesterday when we talked. That reminds me—did you hear anything about that ring we found?"

"Hear anything?"

"Did you talk to Finn about it?"

"No, I didn't. I'm sure he'll update you on anything that's important."

I was almost sure he wouldn't, but I didn't voice that. "I read up about this play tonight," I said. "I wanted to make sure I knew what was going on."

He grinned. "It's not opera. It's all in English."

"Opera?" I shuddered. "Perish the thought."

"This is a pretty simple plot," Royal said, taking the exit for downtown. "Boy meets girl. Boy and girl fall in love. Boy turns out to be a jerk, and they separate. They find each other again and live happily ever after." He hummed something I didn't recognize, a lilting song with lots of highs and lows. "That's the fourth song they'll sing tonight."

"You know the play that well?" I asked. "You know all the songs in it?"

"I told you. It's one of my favorites. What's not to like? Lost love found, triumphing against all odds."

"That's a bit of an over-simplification, don't you think? What about the racial stuff? From what I read, this play set the world on its ear in its day."

"Yeah, there is that aspect," he admitted. "But at the center of the play is the love story between Gaylord and Magnolia. She has to take a chance on him, and she does. At first it doesn't appear that it'll work out." We were at red light, and he looked at me. "It's all about taking chances, isn't it? Love is, I mean."

"I suppose so."

"You don't sound too convinced." He made a left turn into a parking garage near the theater.

"I haven't had much experience with true love. I guess I'm not really sure."

"No one is." He parked the car. "But there is one sure bet, and that is that I think you'll really enjoy this. At least, I hope you do."

We walked out of the garage, walking a short half-block to the theater on the corner. I had never been in this theater, one of three in town used for live entertainment. I had been to the convention center across the street for a Brooks and Dunn concert, and to the Regal a few blocks away for the aforementioned Nutcracker performance.

But this theater, The Crown, was one I never visited because it mainly hosted live theater which I never had a reason to attend—until now. We entered the spacious foyer, a small sitting area on the left and doors leading to the theater itself on the right. From there, we went to the attached dining area through a set of double doors. Twenty or thirty small tables were set up with seating around the perimeter on padded benches. The lighting came from faux candles on the tables, giving the whole place a cozy, warm feeling.

We took a table for two near the windows next to

the street. "There's not much choice on the menu." Royal studied the little placard that sat in a holder next to the table's candle. "It's mainly snacks and appetizers because it's not a restaurant per se but more of a gathering place pre-performance. But I know the caterer. They do a great charcuterie and cheese platter I've been wanting to try."

"Sounds good. Meat and cheese."

"How about a glass of wine?" I nodded. Royal looked up at the waitress, who was beaming at him with more than waitressy happiness.

"Hey, Mr. Royal. It's nice to see you. How's it going?"

"It's going good..." Royal paused.

"Shelly," she supplied. "I was Frenchy in *Grease.*"

"I remember you," Royal said with a smile. "Beauty school dropout."

"That was a fun production." She held up her notepad. "No role for me in this one, so I'm helping out here. What can I get you?"

"We'll have the number four platter with two glasses of the Geisen Riesling." He replaced the placard.

"I'll have that for you in jiffy." She bounced away, the picture of youthful energy.

"They know you here," I said with a grin. "Are you a regular?"

He nodded. "Season ticket holder. I like to support the arts."

I surveyed the room, which was decorated with pictures from the different productions that had been staged. "I've never been here before. Tell me about this theater."

"It's a nice little venue. Seats about five hundred with the balcony. All the performers are volunteers and semi-professional. There's some amazing talent in this community. The prop people and behind-the-scenes people are volunteers, too. I think there's only a dozen or so paid professionals to run the box office, manage the charitable foundation, and do the business stuff." He gestured around the room. "As you can see, it's all vintage decorations. The theater was built in the early 20th century. They've maintained the décor of that era."

"I don't know much about design," I said. "I tend toward an if-it-fits-and-I-like-it-I-buy-it philosophy."

"You obviously have a good eye for design, though. You ran a store that specialized in garden art and gift items."

When did I tell him that? I think I mentioned I ran a store, but did I say what kind? Our wine arrived, and I took a cautious sip. It was dry, thank goodness, and not sweet. I couldn't abide sweet wine. "I think I did the same thing with the shop," I said. "If I liked it, I stocked it. I guess there were enough people around who liked the same kind of stuff, because I didn't have any trouble getting rid of most of it when I had my close-out sale." I had a brief pang of regret when I said those words, then I resolutely pushed it away. If I had still been working, I wouldn't be sitting here with this man, enjoying a glass of wine before a play.

The food arrived, and we sipped and snacked until the lights flickered. "That's our cue," Royal said. "Time to take our seats." He led the way out of the sitting area, and we joined the stream of people filing through the various double doors into the theater. It was, indeed, an ornate old venue with muted green-gray walls and ivory-colored faux columns in plaster at various intervals. A red velvet curtain covered the stage, matching the coverings on the seats.

Our seats were in the center, near the back. "If you don't mind, I'll take the aisle seat." Royal gestured to the two end seats.

I eyed his long legs. "Makes sense to me. How tall are you?"

"Six-four. It makes theater seating a challenge sometimes." We settled down, and I reached into my purse to silence my phone. I spied the receipt there. "I meant to give this to Finn. Someone left this for me at the restaurant. I thought it might have to do with that ring Finn took." I handed him the receipt.

"Who gave you this?" he asked, his head bowed over the paper and his voice so low I barely heard him over the buzz of the audience.

"I don't know. That's what's so weird. Vaughan says I have a secret admirer, but I doubt it's that. I think it was the guy from the bar the other night."

"What guy?" Royal appeared oddly grim, as though all the previous joking and laughter was forgotten.

"When you went to take your phone call. This guy sat down. I think he was a customer from my shop. He said something about not having seen me for a while. Of course, the store has been closed for weeks." I opened the playbill that had been thrust into my hands by the usher. "I suppose I should give that receipt to Finn."

"I'll probably be seeing him," Royal said. "I'll give it to him." He reached under his sweater and tucked the paper into a pocket. His expression was hard to decipher, but I think he appeared puzzled.

"Oh, good. There's a play summary here, too. I guess I didn't need to do any research."

Royal opened his copy of the publication. "They've cut a couple of numbers. I'm not surprised. It runs a bit long when they do the full version." He sat back in his chair, but he seemed distracted, his gaze bouncing around the audience. "There's a challenging duet in the first act for the soprano. We'll see if she's in voice today. And they included a song in the second act that's sometimes skipped because it's a real stretch for some sopranos."

"In voice?" I studied the list of names, but their musical range wasn't listed. "Which is the soprano?"

"Magnolia is the lead soprano. Joe is the bass, Julie is sometimes an alto or contralto."

I turned to regard him. "How do you know so much about it?"

He shrugged. "I've studied music. To answer your question: to be 'in voice' means a singer is prepared to tackle some optional notes. Not every song has to be sung exactly as written. There are some variations a singer can perform that take it over the top. The duet is early in the play, though, and sometimes singers aren't quite warmed up enough to take on the high notes."

Oh, Lord. There it was again. High notes. I sat back, glad that the theater would be dark when those notes were sung. I didn't want anyone to see me cringe.

An usher appeared at the end of our row and handed a folded paper to Royal. "It's good to see you, Mr. Royal," he said with a smile.

Royal nodded then read the note before refolding it and tucking it into his pants pocket. "What is it?" I asked. "Work?"

"No, it's from the theater troupe. They wanted me to stop backstage after the performance. We're old friends. We don't have to go. That's okay."

"No, I'd like to. I've never been behind the scenes at a theater." I'd barely been in a theater, period, but I didn't tell him that. "It might be fun to see what it's like."

"Well, sure. If you want to, we'll stop in. It's been a while since I saw any of them."

"A while?"

"Yeah. I used to act now and then. I played alongside some of them."

I turned to regard him with open-mouthed astonishment. "You acted?" I gestured toward the stage. "Like this? And sang and—and—"

"Yep. I've played Gaylord Ravenal a couple of times." The lights dimmed, and the audience rustled in anticipation.

"But—are you an actor?"

"Hush, now. Play's about to start." He leaned close to me. "Yes, I've been an actor off and on for about forty years. I'll tell you all about it later." He settled back in his seat while the orchestra, situated somewhere in the darkness ahead of us, warmed up with a few soft notes.

I turned to face the stage, my mind in a whirl. A cop and an actor. What was the world coming to? The music started to swell and grow, and I was soon lost in the play, my astonishment at Royal's revelation replaced by my astonishment at the talent I was watching. These weren't professional players? You could have fooled me.

The story got to the part that Royal said was tough. The lead man's voice was powerful, filling the auditorium with each note. The song was the one Royal had hummed earlier, the one with all the high and low notes. I peeked at my program, but it was too dark to make out the words. I made a mental note to check the program later for the song title.

Then the woman—Magnolia—began to sing. I sat up in surprise. Yes, there were high notes, but she enunciated every word in such a way that I leaned forward, anxious to hear. The two singers had voices that blended and contrasted very nicely, with the man singing low notes, the woman singing high ones, and all combining to somehow twine around each other.

When the two sang together, I glanced at Royal. He was watching the performance, a faint smile that told me happy memories were there, just in front of him. I sensed when the song was nearing its climax. Royal's hand stole out and took mine, and he clasped it tightly. The soprano threw back her shoulders and suddenly there it was—on the *you* of *I love you*, she seemed to stretch and lift and reached an impossible note, holding it while she stared into the man's eyes.

Royal's hand tightened on mine. "Good work," he whispered. "Well done."

The audience burst into applause, and I joined them, knowing I had just heard a woman who was beautifully 'in voice.'

Royal and I went into the lobby at half-time, joining hundreds of other patrons of the arts. I was bemused and amazed, I guess. "I had no idea theater could be like this," I confided to Royal.

"Like what?"

"Fun. I thought *The Nutcracker* was kinda boring, but this is fun. There's a plot and everything."

He laughed, the sound carrying over the crowd. "The Nutcracker isn't musical theater," he said. "It's ballet. Musical theater is *West Side Story* or *Carousel* or *Oklahoma.*"

"And *Chicago?*" I remembered seeing ads for the film when it came out. I didn't go because it involved singing and dancing, which I used to think I disliked. I guess my tastes were changing.

He stilled, and for an instant he was flat-out angry, as though someone had jerked him back, hard. "Sure," he said. "*Chicago* and *Grease* and *Rent,* too. They're newer. I don't know them as well."

"Sing something," I said. "Just a little bit."

"What? Not here."

"Come on." I tugged his hand and dragged him outside. It was chilly, and the sidewalk in front of the theater was empty, most people opting to stay inside where it was warm. "Sing something," I prompted. "I've never been up close to a musician before. Sing that one they sang earlier, the one with the high note."

He stared down at me, his eyes intent on mine. Then he began to sing, softly at first, "Only Make Believe." He sang just the first few lines of the song, but when he took my hands and sang, "Couldn't we?" I felt as if the words were traveling down his arms and into my heart.

He pulled me to him, and we fell into the most magical kiss I've ever experienced.

Chapter 8

"That's amazing," I whispered when we pulled apart.

"What is?" He cupped my face in his hands, peering down at me. The lights in the marquee above us dimmed. "Saved by the bell." He kissed me again, this time tenderly but with that sense of banked passion I felt earlier. But when I gazed into his eyes, I saw not excitement but sadness or maybe worry.

Then he put his arm around my shoulders, and we walked back into the theater. I felt like I was on cloud nine, or maybe there wasn't even a cloud there. Maybe I was walking on air. The words of that song, the feeling when he sang it, the night—there really was magic afoot.

Act Two was something I would never forget, not just because of the play but because of how I sat with Royal's arm around me, entranced by the story and by the man beside me. When the curtain went up for the final bows, I was one of the first in the theater on my feet, applauding. I couldn't remember having such a marvelous evening.

We waited for the crowd to thin out then Royal took my hand. We made our way to the front of the theater and the steps leading up to the stage. He pulled aside the heavy velvet curtain, and we stepped into controlled chaos. All sorts of people were bustling around, pulling some of the dozens of ropes at the side of the curtain and tugging scenery this way and that or moving prop furniture to various places. Everything back here was worn and used, not the glitzy and glamorous view we had from the front.

We wended our way among the workers, Royal pausing now and again to greet someone or chat. Eventually we got to an area behind the scenery, a long hallway with doors on each side, leading to a big door labeled *Exit* at the end. Royal ignored all the doors and went to the last one on the right, opening it and stepping inside.

I followed, still holding his hand. We were in a circular room crammed with costumes and furniture. The people from the cast were milling around at a table that held bottles of wine and beer and plates of small sandwiches. When we entered, several people turned. "There he is!" someone called. "We wondered when you'd be back! Good to see you, Bren!"

I lost contact with his hand when Royal was swept into a crowd of well-wishers. Most of the people were still in costume. The man who played Joe in the play spoke with him then moved away when the woman who played Julie came forward.

"Brendan! What are you doing here?" The woman, a light-skinned Black woman, flung her arms around Royal. "Oh, it's so good to see you! When are you coming back?" She drew back to regard him but kept her body pressed against his.

He put his hands on her shoulders and gently unglued her. "No time soon, Rosie. I'm busy right now."

"No, you're not serious." She shook a finger at him

in mock dismay. "Bren, we miss you. It's not the same without you on stage with us." She turned to the man who portrayed Gaylord Ravenal. "Right, Jacob?"

The man nodded, but it appeared more pro-forma than anything. "Sure. There's always room for another baritone."

"We heard that they're staging *Oklahoma* next winter," the woman said. "That's one of our favorites, Bren. Tell me you'll audition. I'd love to be your Laurey again." She smiled in a way that told me exactly what kind of relationship her Laurey would love to have with him.

"Well, it all depends on the timing." Royal kissed her quickly on the cheek then stepped back, putting his arm around my shoulders. "I just wanted to congratulate you on another great performance."

"We're going over to the King for drinks. Can you join us?" The woman finally paid attention to me, her smile perfunctory. "I'm sure your friend would love to meet the rest of the cast."

"No, sorry, we've got to meet some folks," Royal said before I could open my mouth.

The woman—Julie—turned to me. Her stage makeup was so thick I thought it might crack. "Bren's Billy Bigelow in *Carousel* is perfection. There isn't a dry eye in the house when he sings *You'll Never Walk Alone*. He's just the perfect rogue."

"Gaylord? Is that my favorite Gaylord?"

I turned at the lilting voice. It was the woman who played Magnolia, sashaying toward us in her elaborate ball gown and makeup. Up close I could see she was older than I thought. She was still a beautiful woman but starting to fade a bit. Then I gave myself a mental slap upside the head. Who was I to talk?

"There he is, my favorite hero." Her voice had a brittle quality to it that seemed forced. She floated through the throng of people and went up to Royal, enfolding him in a gentle hug then she stepped back. "Are things going good for you?"

"He looks happy," a voice spoke softly behind me.

I turned. The guy who played Joe in the play was watching Royal. "Yeah, I think he is," I said.

"It's a good change from his regular job."

"I suppose," I answered. I hardly heard him. I was watching Royal with Nolie. Their interaction was a little too casual, like friends who pretended not to be friendly.

"I mean, that's stressful. Especially after that thing two years ago."

I finally focused on the man talking to me. "Two years?" I asked, as though questioning the time. "Was it two?"

"Yeah, two years since he had that bullet wound. We weren't sure he'd pull through." 'Joe' frowned. "Maybe that's why he didn't try out for the Ravenal part. Or maybe—" He nodded to the woman who played Magnolia. "I don't think they've been in a play together since the break-up."

Sholey hits, the crap was coming at me fast and furious. Bullet wound? What kind of consulting did Royal do? I struggled to keep up with the flow of information. "I suppose they broke up because of his work," I said in an *I'm on the inside track* tone of voice.

Joe nodded. "It's not every woman who can handle having an FBI agent as a boyfriend—guy friend— whatever. Although to be honest, I think the acting had as much to do with it as the police work. She always likes to be the headliner. There were a few times when he upstaged her. Oh, he didn't mean to, but he's got such a stage presence."

Stage presence? That was one way to phrase it. The guy was a Grade A, Number One liar. I watched Royal talk to people, all easy-going and casual. FBI agent? What else didn't I know? The Joe guy continued to talk. I must have made the correct responses because it appeared to make sense to him. I automatically smiled at Royal when he joined us.

"I see you've met," he said.

"Yep." I surveyed the people around us. "Quite a crowd. Are you sure you don't want to stay?"

"No, we should be going." He put his hand on my arm, but I managed to slip away from him by turning as though I wanted to smile at someone near the door. Royal followed me, still chatting with people.

We made it to the hallway, and Royal pointed to the exit door. "We can go out this way. It opens right into the alley next to the parking garage. That way we don't have as far to walk outside." He pushed open the door. I slipped through, hurrying across the chilly and damp alley into the garage. I kept a foot or two in front of him until we got to the garage.

"You've been in plays before?" I asked while we walked through the misty evening.

"Yeah, a few."

"A baritone? You played the lead?"

"A few times. Like I said, I like the old ones the best, but I've done some newer ones, too. I've done Daddy Warbucks in *Annie*, Professor Higgens in *My Fair Lady,* Curly in *Oklahoma.*" He shrugged then dipped his chin into his upturned collar. "A few."

"Why didn't you do it full-time? Professionally?" I got to his SUV and waited for him to unlock the door for me with his key fob. I had the door open and I got inside before he could come around and open the door for me.

He got into the driver's side and started the car. "Are you okay?"

"Fine. I just feel cold all of a sudden." I used that excuse to bury my chin in my jacket collar, effectively hiding my face. "So why don't you act full-time?"

He didn't answer until we got out to the street. "I decided I didn't want to pursue it like that. If I did, it would be a job. I wanted it to be fun. You can be excellent at something, but it doesn't have to be your career."

"And you and her—Nolie?" I nodded when I saw his surprised expression. "That guy who played Joe mentioned that you and she were an item."

"We had a relationship for a time," Royal said. "A few years ago."

"What happened?"

"I don't know. There just wasn't a connection, a spark." He flashed that wry smile. "I guess like doesn't always attract like. And it can be tough when you're both focusing on a career. Acting takes a lot of time, and so does my day job."

His day job. I stared out my window, anger slowly bubbling in me. What was real and what was a lie? I thought about that kiss we shared outside the theater. "You're a good actor," I said, thinking out loud.

"What?"

"That's what everybody said. You're a good actor.

Did you have training? I mean, did someone teach you how to sing like that and act like that?"

"I started acting and singing when I was in high school. There's a lot of training involved." He started to hum, his voice resonant and strong.

"It must be a huge time commitment. You probably have to go to rehearsals and learn scripts and all that."

"It is. Most plays require four hours each evening for rehearsals, sometimes more. We used to rehearse for the month before an opening. Then the play would run for a month or so, with four or more performances a week."

"A huge commitment. Lots of training."

"Yes." He glanced at me. "I suppose it is."

"Sort of like the commitment and training to be an FBI agent?" I flashed him a bright and insincere smile.

The car was suddenly quiet. "You found out."

"Yeah." I moved as far away from him as I could. "I found out."

"It's not what you think."

"You have no idea what I think," I said, my voice cool and level.

He was quiet for a long minute. I could see him considering and discarding what to say in the way his eyes flickered between traffic and me. He finally said, "Talk to your friend, Finn Sterling."

"Finn? He's in on this?" I retrieved my purse from the footwell where I'd stowed it and jerked it open to fumble for my phone. I turned it on, and immediately the *Missed Call* icon and the *Message* icons flashed. I checked the phone number of the missed call.

"Great minds think alike," I snapped. "He's been trying to call me." I opened the text icon. Yep, it was from Finn. *Call me ASAP. Important.* I opened my contact list and tapped his name.

He answered on the first ring. "Where are you?"

"I'm on the way to my house with the guy who's pretending to be my date."

There was a long pause. "Put Special Agent Royal on the phone."

"The hell I will."

"Do it, Snow. Now." This was Calm, the man who had won the college baseball tournament by hitting a bottom of the ninth home run that clinched the game. He walked up to the plate, stared at the pitcher, and took the first pitch thrown at him. The ball went sailing into the stands. Finn slowly jogged around the bases as though it was an everyday occurrence while everyone in the stands went crazy. Nothing fazed him or annoyed him. To hear the anger in those four words made me realize how serious this was.

"He wants to talk to you." I held out the phone.

Royal—no, Agent Royal—turned into a side street and pulled the car over to the curb, taking the phone from me. He jammed the gear lever into park and put the phone to his ear. "What happened?" he asked. "No, she doesn't know it all." He listened to Finn. I ignored him, staring fixedly out my window. I heard Finn's voice, very faintly, on the phone, then Royal said, "Okay. We'll see you there." He handed me the phone.

I tapped the *End* icon and dropped it back in my purse, resuming my stare-out-the-window ploy.

"Your friend Brian is unconscious," Royal said. "His wife, Paulina, is dead."

"Oh, my God." My stomach, already doing flip-flops, flopped some more. "Nimble and Sporty?" I croaked. "What happened?"

"I'd rather wait to talk about it. Deputy Sterling will meet us at your house. We'll get the complete update then." Royal stared ahead, his face tense.

Okay. I could play that game.

Ten minutes later we pulled into my driveway. Finn's sedan was parked in front of the shop. As soon as our headlights appeared, both Finn and Vaughan jumped out of Finn's car. Finn carried several file folders, tucked under his arm.

I got out my house keys and was out of Royal's car before either Finn or Vaughan could reach me. I strode up the front walk, managed to get the door open, and went inside, flinging my purse at the couch. Mr. Gold took one look at me, and he ran. I suspected Miss Copper was already hiding under the bed.

I turned to face the three men entering my house. "Somebody had better start talking fast." I didn't wait for a reply. Instead, I went to the kitchen and snatched a wine glass from the cupboard. I went to the Wine in a Box I had on the counter and filled it with cheap red wine. Then I came back to the living room to glare at them.

Vaughan winced when he saw my face. "Snow, we thought it was best that—"

I held up my hand and took a swallow of the wine. Then I turned to Finn. "What happened to Nimble and Sporty?"

Finn came into the living room. His shoulders sagged, and his face was pale and haggard. He walked to the floor lamp that was on next to the couch and turned it off. Then he went to the lamp at the far end of the room and turned it to its dimmest setting. I didn't bother questioning his odd behavior. It was just one more odd thing in a long list.

He turned to me. "It was a self-driving car. We thought Brian was driving because he was behind the wheel, but he wasn't. He was unconscious when he was put in the car. And Paulina—" Finn hesitated.

"What?" I shifted my attention to Royal. His face was like a mask, his eyes revealing nothing of what he thought. I turned to Finn. "What?"

"She was strangled and put in the car. She was murdered before they even left their house."

Somehow, I wasn't shocked. All the little odd things from the last few days started to make sense. Finn, acting so odd. Vaughan insisting on me finding "Mr. Right Now." Royal, defending Finn's odd behavior. Even the coincidence of all the women in our group dying.

All the women except me.

"Snow?" Royal's voice was gentle, almost kind. "Are you —"

"You don't get to call me that." I kept my voice as steady as I could. "I'm Natalie DeWitt to you."

Royal flinched as if I'd hit him. "I never lied to you."

"But you never told me the truth."

His lips twisted in a half-smile. "Shades of gray. Coming from a woman who only wears black, white, and gray."

I went to the window and stared at the yard outside. I could only make out the silhouette of trees. Clouds covered the moon, and the darkness was complete. "And red. Don't forget the red." The word reminded me of the glass in my hand. I took three gulps of wine and set the glass on the end table. I was afraid if I held it any longer I might throw it at him.

"Right." His voice was as cool as mine.

"Who is it?" I asked. "Who's doing it?"

Royal pulled a phone out of his back pocket and stared down at it, swiping at various icons. He stepped forward and held up the phone in front of me.

I stared at the photo. It was a bit blurry, like it was part of a larger picture and had been cropped and enlarged. "I don't know who that is."

"Examine it closely."

I took the phone. The man had a gaunt, almost skeletal face with a deep scar on the left side that caused his left eye to droop. His eyes were the palest blue and so devoid of expression it was eerie, like he was a mannequin or puppet. I handed the phone back. "I don't know him."

"It's Hunter Mann," Finn said.

I looked at him, then at Vaughan, who nodded. "Hunter Mann? From college? The guy who attacked me?" I finally turned to Royal. He nodded, too. "That can't be him."

"Why not?"

"He was the prettiest boy. We all said he could have been a movie star. He was like one of those old timey stars, like Troy Donahue or some surfer boy." I shook my head. "Are you sure that's him?"

Finn nodded.

"That's not the guy from the bar—either bar," I said. "You must be wrong."

"He has associates," Finn said. "He's lost a lot of weight. He's noticeable now. He probably sent one of his people in his place."

"What happened to him?"

"Prison," Royal said.

I took a step back. "What?"

"He was sentenced to ten years and sent to a prison in Illinois, on a reciprocity program. There's a hierarchy in prison, and rapists are just slightly higher than pedophiles. Inmates love pretty boys. From what I can piece together, a gang used him as their sex toy for a few years. Then he killed one of them and got another ten years for justifiable homicide."

I sank down on the couch, my knees so wobbly I was sure I'd collapse if I didn't. "I didn't know. My God, I never expected anything like that to—"

"It's not your fault." Vaughan sat next to me, giving me a brief hug. "He raped those girls, and he tried to rape you. He deserved what happened to him."

"Actually, he ended up on top." Royal still stood near the doorway to the living room as though unsure if he should come in any farther or not.

"What do you mean?" I could only imagine the horror of being in a prison and being abused like that. It was nightmarish.

"He murdered the leader of the gang that was using him and became their de facto leader. By the time he got out of prison, he had quite an operation going. Illegal gun sales, drugs, prostitution. He started in Chicago and moved on to other cities."

Chicago. Is that why Royal reacted so oddly when I mentioned it earlier? I shook my head. What did that matter? I had more important things to worry about. "But why now? Why is he taking revenge now if he's a successful underworld kingpin of some kind? If what you say is true, he got out of prison years ago." I did some fast math. "He's been out for, what, ten or fifteen years? What was he waiting for?"

Royal's expressive green eyes took on a hooded, secretive appearance. "He didn't wait. He's been killing all along."

"What? That's crazy! If you had somebody killing women for twenty years, why didn't you spot him?" I stared at Finn as I spoke. I wasn't sure how I felt about Royal except for being pissed off at his lies. It felt safer to talk through Finn.

"At first they seemed like accidents or natural causes. It wasn't until a few years ago that the FBI discovered those weren't accidents at all." Finn walked into the living room, his hands jammed into his coat pockets. He moved to the window, standing on my left. Vaughan was still on my right, and it felt as if they were protecting me—from Royal? From the truth?

I stared at him in open-mouthed astonishment. "You didn't figure it out?"

"We didn't connect the dots until recently when he began to rape and murder them. They were women from all walks of life, all locations, with no common thread."

"Except college athletics," I murmured.

"It took a long time to find the commonality," Royal admitted in a harsh, tortured voice. "Scholarship records aren't kept active for more than ten years. We had to track down people who remembered the coach, who remembered the other team members."

"Which is how you found me."

"That and other things. Once we figured they were all affiliated with NMU, we had a starting point. We began to backtrack, reviewing all the women's sports.

Keep in mind, we're trying to figure out team rosters and details from thirty-some years ago. It was hit or miss a lot of the time. Nothing's online. It's all buried in scrapbooks in the attic or on microfilm."

"What did you find?"

"The two girls who testified against him were dead. One died in a car accident ten years ago. The other died in an accident at her home. She fell off a ladder." Finn's flat, unemotional voice told me what he thought of these deaths.

"Who else?"

Royal pulled a folded piece of paper from his inside coat pocket, hesitating before coming into the room to hand it to me. "Holy Besus in a jucket," I whispered, staring at the list of names. Each had a year and an initial next to it: M, CA, RM, HA, NC. "What do they mean?"

"Mugging, car accident, rape/murder, home accident, natural causes."

I counted the names. "There are eighteen women on this list."

Royal nodded. "All scholarship athletes from spring sports. There were twenty scholarships given out to females for spring sports that year. One of the women died from cancer a few years out of college. Another one was killed in a plane accident about ten years after your graduation."

I scanned the list. "Oh," I breathed. "There's Bitchy and Brainy." There was a CA next to Charlene's name and a RM next to Heidi's.

"He escalated in the last six years. He's not taking one each year. Some years there were two, and one year there was three. That's why there are so many RM cases, one after another. He doesn't care anymore."

"Escalated?" My hands were trembling so bad I lowered the paper. "Doesn't care? But why? He's done this for so long. Why now?"

"We think that's when he found out he had AIDS."

"What?" I added nausea to my overall trembling.

"He quit trying to cover his tracks. He's dying. We have test results from evidence he's left behind. He has an advanced case of AIDS. He probably got HIV in prison and was never tested for it."

I stared from Finn to Vaughan. I still couldn't look at Royal. "How could someone kill twenty people and not be found out?"

Royal took a step forward. "The Garden State killer raped and murdered people for decades. Our last count was fifty-seven victims of either rape or murder or both." Royal almost spat the words, as though they left a bad taste in his mouth. "Ted Bundy killed at least thirty-five people before he was found out. William Bonin, the Freeway Killer, murdered twenty-one young men that we could prove. Believe me, if there was some fast way to figure out who's a serial killer, I'd like to know about it. The way it stands now, it's like putting together a jigsaw puzzle with all the edge pieces missing. We never know what connects them until we find that one key piece."

"What was the key piece in this case?" I handed him the paper, which he folded and tucked back into his pocket. I knew what he would say before he spoke.

"The trophies. We didn't see it at first."

"You mean he took—" I swallowed hard. "Things from the women he killed?"

Royal nodded as though this was the most natural

thing in the world. I suppose it was natural in his world. "They were small things. We didn't figure it out until six or seven years ago. He took something from each victim—an earring, or a necklace or a ring—and he left it at his next victim. When we found that victim, we found the connection to the previous one." He nodded to Finn.

Finn went to the manila folder he carried into the house and opened it. He pulled out a picture and handed it to me. "Do you recognize this?"

I examined the photo. It was a short gold trophy with the figure on top that of a woman, crouched with her hands upraised. "I don't understand. It's an award but—"

"Something's missing." Finn pointed to the figure's hands. "She should be holding a baseball bat."

"Where did you find it?"

"Sporty's house. It was ransacked, but she and Nimble didn't think anything was taken. It was the day before they flew out here. They didn't have time to do a complete inventory. The FBI investigators found it." He drew out another photo and placed it on top of the one I still held.

I stared down at what appeared to be a small gold baseball bat. "Where did you find it?"

"In her suitcase. Someone put it there before they left their home. He puts a trophy from his previous victim with his next victim. That's from a woman who was murdered last year. She had a softball trophy. He took the bat from her trophy and he left it with Sporty."

I sat down, suddenly drenched in a cold sweat. "Sporty's ring." The words came out in a croak as my throat closed up. "The one I found in my shop. He put it there so I'd find it. Dear God. I can't believe this is happening."

"Believe it, Snow. You're the last one. You're next."

Chapter 9

"We didn't want you to know," Finn said. "We didn't want to worry you."

"We wanted you to act natural," Royal said. "If you knew, you might act defensive. That might tip him off, and things could get out of hand."

"Are you crazy? Of course, I'd act defensive. Somebody is trying to kill me. Why wouldn't I be defensive?" I shook my head. "Fut the wuck, you guys are insane."

"Would you please just swear like a regular person?" Vaughan snapped. "It gives me a headache trying to translate you."

I glared at him. "Fuck. Off," I enunciated.

"It's just—you're so trusting. We were afraid that if you acted out of character, that would alert him. If he thinks you're unsuspecting, then they can trap him. You don't have anything to worry about."

"Nothing to worry about?" I stared at Vaughan. "Are you crazy?"

"We figured if you had someone with you, you'd be okay." Finn nodded at Royal.

"Oh, thanks," I snarled. "Way to make me feel better." I turned on Royal. "What about tonight? Was that all part of —" I held up my hands. "This?"

"Tonight?" Finn swung around to face Royal. "What happened?"

"Nothing happened," Royal snapped.

"He kissed me." I glared at Royal. "Was that all part of your disguise? I suppose all your acting lessons really paid off, didn't they? It made it easy to act like you cared."

Royal stared at me, his eyes so cold I was surprised ice chips didn't shoot out. "I don't get involved with clients," he said, his voice as frosty as his eyes. "That might distract me. If I get distracted, you might get killed. The most important thing is keeping you safe."

"It seems like you've failed pretty miserably. I mean, you knew this guy was out there. How long did you know who he was? How long have you known all of this?"

Finn held up his hand, probably worried I was going to take a swing at somebody. "They did the best they—"

"Why didn't you protect Sporty? Why didn't you protect the other women who died? How long have you known about this?"

"We weren't sure." Royal's face was so rigid, so tense, it was like it was carved from rock.

"For how long?" I demanded.

"We weren't sure," Royal repeated. "A few months ago, we decided to notify the police in the towns where we thought there might be a target. Don't forget, all we had were incomplete lists and fragments of memory from decades ago. Any of a dozen or more women might be targets or they might not be. It wasn't clear-cut. We weren't sure if it was just scholarship athletes or all female athletes. Was it spring sports or all sports? We didn't have rosters or lists or any way to be certain."

A target. That's what I was. A target.

"We got lucky. Deputy Sterling saw the alert. He put the pieces together."

"How?" I asked Finn. Then I saw Vaughan's panicked expression. "What?"

"I—I saw it," Vaughan stammered. "I recognized some of the names." He glanced apologetically at Finn, who sighed. "Finn was rooting around in the attic, trying to find some old yearbooks and things. We kind of argued about it."

"No, we did argue," Finn corrected. "I told you it wasn't any of your business. It was police business. You were not supposed to interfere."

"But it had to do with college, so I thought I could help." Vaughan glared defiantly at Royal, as though the FBI agent had voiced his own criticism. "I know I'm just a civilian and I don't know about police procedure and stuff like that, but it seemed important. Then when I saw the names I—"

"You knew some of the girls on the list?" I asked. "How?"

"Two of the girls played tennis. I practiced with them. And—" he hesitated then said in a rush, "Back then, not very many queer folks were out of the closet. One of the girls who played softball was gay. She and I became friends. I saw her name on the list."

"And he demanded to know why I had a list of female athletes from our old school," Finn said with a wry smile. "It was Vaughan who figured it out."

"Jesus Christ on a skateboard," I breathed. "Finn, if you hadn't become a cop…"

He nodded. "We might never have put it together."

"Deputy Sterling was pulled into the investigation.

That led us to your friend in Florida." Royal's shoulders, already rigidly straight, seemed to pull back. Finn shot him a brief frosty look.

"What happened? If you were watching out for Sporty, how did this crazy guy get to her? How did he kill her?"

"It wasn't that simple."

"Not that simple?" I rounded on Royal, my fists clenched. "Crazy guy is threatening women. You know he's out there. You protect them. End of story."

"We had police patrolling the area," Royal said. "The officers were killed. Their bodies were found this morning."

I stepped back, as if moving away from him might distance me from this violence. Vaughan took my arm and led me back to the couch, where I sat down with a thump.

"Don't forget. Mann runs a crime ring. He has resources." Royal sounded dispassionate, but I saw the cold fire in his green eyes. "It was a professional hit. Sniper. Long distance."

"Oh, my God," I breathed. "What is happening?"

"We knew he'd come after you and her and maybe some others. We just weren't sure when. But then you got her ring, so we made sure your friend in Florida was protected. We were too late, though. He was already moving."

"And now I'm next." Did I even say the words out loud? My head was spinning. I sucked in a long, ragged breath, then I raised my head to regard the three men all watching me. "Okay. What now? How do we catch him?"

"You don't get involved," Royal said.

"Too late, Sherlock. I'm in this up to my neck." I kept my eyes on them, but my mind was going a thousand miles an hour. "You got close to me to protect me. That way, between you and Finn and—are there cops watching me? Watching the house?" I twisted to peer behind me through the windows at the woods surrounding my property.

"Now we do." Royal and Finn exchanged a look, sharing some unspoken message between them. "We won't be able to pretend anymore," Royal said. "If he's watching her, then he's seen you here. He knows you're with the sheriff's office. We can't play it out."

"What's that mean?" I demanded.

Vaughan shook his head warningly. "It's cop business. Let them manage it."

"Manage what?"

"They were hoping Mann didn't know Special Agent Royal was with the FBI."

"Vaughan." Finn's quiet voice made Vaughan wince.

"Sorry." Vaughan grimaced. "Cop business."

"It's my business, too." I bounced to my feet. I would *not* let them keep me out of this any longer. "You were hoping anybody seeing us wouldn't know that he was a cop, right? Why? Why wouldn't they know that? Isn't this guy a hotshot criminal?"

"I'm not on regular duty here," Royal said.

"Oh, you're a special Special Agent?" I glared at him, wishing I had the nerve to hit him or yell at him or something that involved physical action. All I could do was stare at him with my fists clenched.

"I was sent here to recover after an accident a couple of years ago. A temporary assignment became a permanent one at my request. But I'm still not listed on the roster here."

A bullet wound accident? One glance at Finn's cautionary face and I decided not to pursue the topic. "You were hoping you'd pass as a guy friend, right?" I rounded on Vaughan. "That's why you were so anxious to find Mr. Right Now. You should have told me."

He shrugged. "Cop business."

"That's not going to work anymore," Royal said.

"Why not?" I regarded each of them in turn. "As far as anybody knows, two of my oldest friends came over to give me horrible news about my other friends." I trembled with anger, fear, disappointment, and more fear. I couldn't tell which emotion had precedent. It didn't matter. "And Special Agent Royal, a.k.a. My Guy Friend, stayed to comfort me. Believe me, I don't want you here. But I want to catch that bastard more than I'm mad at you."

"That wouldn't be smart," he said.

"Why not?" I challenged. "It would add to the myth of a guy friend."

Finn nodded, his face thoughtful. "It would be good to have someone in place."

"Let's face it. He thinks I'm a slut already. It would make sense to him that I'd have a man stay over when I've just met him."

"Unless he did research on you recently," Vaughan pointed out. "You're hardly a slut."

"His bad opinion of me won't change," I said confidently. "Once a slut, always a slut." I turned to Royal. "You can camp out on the couch tonight. He's probably going to act fast, isn't he? This won't be a long-term thing. He's going to come after me soon?"

"We don't know," Finn said just as Royal said, "Yeah. Probably."

Finn shrugged. "It's hard to say."

Royal shook his head. "It seems like he always acted within a day, maybe two, from the time the victims received the trophy piece. I think it'll be sooner rather than later."

"If he sticks to his previous methods," Finn said. The two men locked gazes.

"He will," Royal said. "He's had a mission. Now it's wrapping up."

There was tension of some kind going on, and I didn't want to get in the middle of it. Maybe it was a 'local-police-versus-Feds' authority thing. That wasn't my problem. They'd have to work out the details of their pissing contest someplace else.

"Let's take it a day at a time," I said. "Finn, we were all getting together tomorrow night anyway, so that's covered. We'll just have to figure out how to cover tomorrow during the day." I smiled wryly. "No one would believe that much togetherness."

Royal met my gaze then nodded once. "I'll coordinate that with the office." He moved to one side and pulled out his phone. Finn followed him.

"This is a mess." Vaughan tugged me across the room toward the hallway leading to the back part of the house. "None of this was supposed to happen."

"None of what?" I peeked over my shoulder at Royal, who was on the far side of the living room. His eyes were fixed on me while he talked on his phone. "I wasn't supposed to be wined and dined by an FBI agent?"

"No, no, that was supposed to happen. I mean, you

were supposed to get comfortable with him. We were hoping that while you were with him, maybe Mann would make his move. And if Special Agent Royal was with you then—"

"Quit calling him that," I hissed. "I hate it."

Vaughan drew back as though I spit. "That's his title."

"I don't call Finn 'Deputy' and I'll be damned if I call him 'Special Agent.' " I crossed my arms, resisting the urge to check and see if Royal was still watching me. "I was the bait, is that it? I was supposed to draw out this freak maniac. Hopefully while the crazy guy was stalking me, the FBI agent would figure it out and save me?"

"When you phrase it like that, it does sound kind of stupid, but it was the best plan they could figure short of staking you out someplace and waiting to see what happened." Vaughan's worried, hang-dog expression only added to my annoyance.

"This whole thing is crazy. I suppose his profile on that dating site was all a lie, too."

"No, it wasn't." I turned. Royal had snuck up behind me. "It's no more a lie than yours was."

I shrugged. "I have no idea what mine was because I didn't do it. I told you that. And now I know why. It was all a setup." I brushed by him to go to the living room, scooping up my wine glass as I went. "You and I are about as compatible as oil and water." I went to the kitchen for a refill.

Finn followed me. "You can't blame him for what happened to Nimble and Sporty." He watched me fill my glass from the spigot, his eyes fixed on my face.

"I can blame him for any damn thing I want." I

reached for the light switch, but Finn put his hand over mine.

"Don't. I'd rather not advertise every move we make in here."

"I thought you said you had guys watching the house?"

"We do. We don't know if he does, too."

"Good Lord, you make it sound like there's a convention going on outside." I took a swallow of wine. My hand was steadier than before. Maybe I was getting accustomed to the idea of being the target of a madman. Or maybe the wine was kicking in. "How long, Finn? Really? How long before he makes his move?" I leaned against the counter, peering at him in the fragments of light that came in from the living room.

"A day. Maybe two. He's sick. We're almost certain that he has cancer and a form of dementia. That happens in late-stage AIDS patients. We think he has a couple of trusted lieutenants who will probably inherit his organization when he dies. They've been with him since he was in prison."

Nausea roiled my stomach again. "I can't imagine that. I know he deserved to be punished, but it's terrible to think of anyone enduring such misery, such abuse."

Finn was quiet for a minute, then he said, "Human beings are capable of some of the most atrocious things I've ever seen, things I can't tell anybody about. I've also seen people do amazing things to help other people. The most I can hope for is that it all balances out, and usually it does. He was treated horrifically, it's true. But he was a predator. If he had remained outside prison, he would have continued assaulting women."

He was right. I knew that. But I still felt that

gnawing sense of guilt. My testimony and the testimony of the other girls was what put him behind bars and set him on this path of murder and violence.

"Don't forget what came out at his trial." Finn put an arm around my shoulders, pulling me to him in a brief hug. "He had a history of abuse. Previous employers said they got complaints about him. Former classmates said the same thing. You didn't set him on this path. He was going to end up there eventually."

"You're probably right." I didn't agree with him, but I knew if I said it, it would make him feel better. "I just wish he could have been stopped sooner." I rested my head on Finn's shoulders, my eyes hot with tears. "Sporty and Brainy and Bitchy. All those other girls. Good God, Finn. What makes a person do that?"

"He's right." Royal spoke from the doorway where he stood, watching us. "Some people are bad to the bone. They might have the best upbringing and the most loving parents and they'll still end up bad. And other kids come from hell environments and go on to help others and improve the world. You didn't cause this. It happened. You and the others got caught up in his ugliness."

"We'd better get going." Vaughan peered around Royal. "If anybody's watching, I doubt if we'd stay long."

"Then let's make it look good." I ushered Vaughan and Finn to the door, then pulled it open. I put my arms around Vaughan's neck. "I wish none of this had ever happened," I said softly.

He hugged me tightly. "You may as well wish that bastard had never been born." He kissed my cheek then peered into my eyes. "Try to get some rest. I know it won't be easy but try. I feel better knowing you have a guard dog with you tonight. I still think he's Mr. Right."

"You're an incurable romantic."

I released him and hugged Finn while we walked out the door, Royal behind us. "I'm sorry this is happening," Finn said. "But we have him now. There's no way he'll get close to you. We'll get him."

I thought of Sporty. Yeah, there was no way he should have been able to get her, either. I didn't voice the thought. I watched Vaughan and Finn walk to their car. "Check the shop, would you?" I called out. "Make sure it's locked?"

Finn gave a wave and tried the door on the shop. "All secure."

"Thanks! I'll see you guys tomorrow."

Royal slipped his arm around my shoulder and gave me a squeeze. "We need to make it look good." He put on a sympathetic expression.

"Right." I slid away from him and went back inside. Royal followed, pulling the door closed and locking it.

"I'll get you a pillow and blanket." I went down the hall to my bedroom, not bothering to wait for his reply. When I saw the bedside clock, I was surprised to see it was almost midnight. As though it was a trigger, exhaustion hit me. I yawned, amazed that I could be considering sleep after everything that had happened. I gazed longingly at my bed, but I was sure if I did lie down, I would probably toss and turn.

I went back to the living room. Royal had turned off the lights. The only illumination came from the faint nightlight over the stove in the adjoining room. He stood near the window, peering out. It was dark, with no moon showing. I was familiar with the silhouettes there, but I suppose he was trying to decipher what he saw.

I tossed the pillow and blanket on the couch. "It's a cold night to be outside watching somebody's house. How many are out there?"

Royal moved away from the window. "Four in alternating shifts." He went to his jacket, which lay on the armchair, and pulled out a phone charger cord. "I'm sorry this had to happen to you. No one deserves this kind of thing."

"You mean being stalked by a serial killer? No, but I suppose it's better for you that he's not some random freak picking people with the roll of a dice."

Royal straightened from plugging in his phone, setting it on the end table near the couch. "Better for us? Maybe. Serial killers have preferences, patterns. Some are easier to see than others."

I thought about that. "You weren't kidding when you said you have to associate with a nasty class of people."

His face was unreadable in the dark. "I've done it for a long time. You never get used to it."

There was nothing to say to that. I turned to go to my bedroom but changed direction and headed for the basement steps. "Where are you going?" he asked.

"Checking the locks downstairs."

"I'll do it."

"I should. It's something I would do."

He crossed the room to me. "We'll both do it."

I led the way down the basement steps, going to the door leading outside. Mr. Gold sat on the couch on the opposite side of the room, eyeing Royal with wary alertness. I glimpsed Miss Copper, hiding under the couch, her tail peeking out. I checked the lock while Royal watched me then we both went back upstairs. "I'll be done in the bathroom in a minute. Use the towels hanging there. Good night." I took my purse and went to my bedroom without a backward glance.

I changed into sweatpants and a baggy T-shirt. It wasn't my usual sleep attire, but I wasn't going to put on a nightie in case I had to bolt out of bed in the middle of the night. I went to the bathroom and washed my face, plaiting my hair into a loose sleep braid. Then I settled under the bedcovers and picked up my red purse, emptying it out and transferring my phone, wallet, and essentials to my everyday bag. I saw the playbill from earlier in the evening. I turned on the bedside light and leafed through it.

Royal was listed among the donors in the 'Spotlight' category—those people who gave a thousand dollars a year or more. There were pages of people listed as donors of various levels, plus volunteers, cast members, and office people. I set the book aside and stared at the wall, marveling at how much effort it took to produce one play. Time and effort and people.

I picked up my phone, but I was too punchy to play any stupid online game. I needed a pill if I was going to get any sleep. I padded into the bathroom and swallowed an over-the-counter sleepy aid then went to the kitchen for some wine.

"I thought you liked beer."

The voice in the living room was muffled. I peered through the darkness, finally making out Royal's shape on the couch. He was propped up, his legs outstretched while he lay against one of the couch cushions set against the couch arm.

I went into the kitchen and filled my glass. "I do. But I don't drink it before bed because of the pee factor." I leaned in the doorway. "So I have wine at night."

"Pee factor?"

"You know. If I drink beer, I pee. So I have a glass of wine instead of a couple of beers."

"That's not wine," he said. "It's a red liquid pretending to be wine."

"Oh, great. A wine snob."

"It's not snobbery to like a good burgundy wine."

"Snob," I muttered.

Royal sneezed. I paused on my way back to my bedroom. "Are you okay?"

He dabbed at his nose with a handkerchief. "I have a mild allergy to cats. I didn't bring any allergy pills with me."

I went into my bathroom and found the bottle of OTC allergy tablets. I went back to the living room and tossed it to him. It landed on his chest with a rattle. "Non-drowsy kind," I said. "Help yourself."

"Thanks."

I started back to the bedroom, but I paused. I doubted if he could explain it, but I still wanted some answers. "I don't understand. Why is he doing this?"

"Prison can do a lot to a person."

"I get that. But why us? Why pick on us?"

"You represent something to him."

"I don't get it."

"You can't. You'd have to think like him to

understand."

"Do you get it?"

Royal was quiet for a long time. "Yeah, I do."

"You can think like him?"

"I know what motivates him."

I was silent, digesting that. I sank into the armchair near the doorway. "Have you always been able to do that, or does the FBI train you to do it?"

"A bit of both."

"Like singing. Talent plus training."

"I guess so."

I thought about it. "That guy said you were shot. He said you had a bullet wound."

Royal sighed. "I really need to talk to him about that. It's not a big deal."

"It's a big deal to people who aren't in law enforcement," I pointed out. "What's it like? I mean, how does it feel to be shot?"

"It's like any injury. It hurts like crazy at first then they give you drugs so it doesn't hurt. Then it hurts like crazy again."

"Where were you shot?"

"In the side. It was a through and through."

I had watched enough police shows to know what that meant. "So you were lucky."

"Yeah. It missed a few important organs on its way out."

"Is that the only time you were shot?"

"What is this, a job interview? Are you worried I'm not a capable guard or something?" I heard the amusement in his voice even though I couldn't see his face.

"It's weird. You live in a different world than I live

in."

"It's not really that much different. I just probably have a lot more fear than you have."

"You?"

He laughed softly. "Yeah, me. Whenever somebody points a gun at me, I'm scared."

"How do you handle it? What do you do?"

He was quiet for a minute. "I try to decide whether I want to point a gun back and what the consequences will be if I do. It's hard to kill someone. It's not an easy choice."

"Where did you learn to do it? To fire a gun? Did you go into the FBI from college? Was it a career choice?"

"This is a job interview, isn't it? No, I was in the Army. I volunteered right out of high school. I wasn't sure what to do with my life. I figured four years in the Army would help me figure it out." He laughed ruefully. "Yeah, right."

"I don't understand people who volunteer for stuff like that," I confessed. "Finn said he enjoys the challenge but the danger—I don't understand it."

"It's a job," Royal said. "The same thing as a garbage collector or a doctor or a plow driver does a job."

"But your job is dangerous, and it protects other people. That's kind of heroic."

"No, not really. I know some guys think it is, but it's a job. I volunteered to do it. I get paid to do it. I'm not a hero."

I wasn't sure about that, but I didn't argue. "That's where you learned to shoot a gun and chase people?"

"I learned about guns in the Army. I found out I

was good with guns. The chasing people part came later. Law enforcement training is designed to help you make good decisions in bad situations." He shifted position, and I saw him more clearly. "Deputy Sterling was right. Don't blame yourself for this."

"What?"

"I've seen it before. Victims blame themselves. Our culture always blames the woman like she was responsible for inciting a man to attack her. But I can choose not to act on my wants and desires. It doesn't matter if a woman is sexy or comes on to me or if she wears short skirts and tight sweaters. I can choose not to react. That's why rapists put the blame on their victims. They don't want to be guilty of choosing to act. They pretend it's out of their control. But everyone chooses their actions. Only victims are coerced into believing their guilt."

"It's very pervasive," I murmured. "It's everywhere."

"I know. I've seen it before. You're not to blame for any of this. It's all on him."

"I still can't believe you sing and act." I paused. "And catch serial killers."

"Everybody needs a hobby. What about you? You said you do sculptures and painting. The theater always needs people to volunteer behind the scenes."

"Me? Work at the theater?"

"Why not? You know how to paint and design things, right? That's what you said."

"Well, yeah. I suppose I could." I stood, glass of wine in hand.

"I meant what I said earlier. I don't want to be distracted by you. When this is over, that's different.

But for now I'm a professional. I'm on the job, and I'm not going to do anything that'll put you in danger. This isn't like one of those romance novels where the FBI guy falls for the girl and drops into bed with her and everything goes to hell because of it."

"I don't read romance novels."

"I'm not saying it's not going to happen," he continued. "I'm just saying it's not going to happen right now. In fact, I think you can take that to the bank."

"Which part?" I asked, intrigued in spite of myself. "The falling in love part or the dropping into bed part?"

Royal laughed softly. "You decide." Then his voice got serious. "I meant what I said."

"I know."

"No. I meant the kiss. That wasn't acting. None of it was."

I studied him in the darkness, his face only a vague shape near the window. "Thanks." I walked down the hall to the bedroom.

"Good night, Snow," he said behind me.

Chapter 10

I drank the wine and finally lay down in bed, but I don't think I really slept. I dozed, woke, worried, dozed, and listened. At about four in the morning I did finally sleep for a time — until I heard something in the hallway.

I sat upright in bed, my heart pounding. The memories of the previous night flooded back. They mingled with the remnants of a dream about someone outside my old store, watching me. Who was out there? No, wait. It was probably Royal. I slipped out of bed and jammed my feet into my bunny slippers, then dragged on my flannel shirt over my T-shirt.

My bedside clock read seven a.m. It was getting light outside with a faint tinge of brightness in my east-facing window. I tiptoed into the hallway and peeked around the doorframe into the kitchen. Royal stood at my refrigerator, peering inside. Mr. Gold was at his feet, staring upward hopefully.

Royal straightened when he saw me. "Good morning."

"Did the pills help?" I snapped my fingers. Mr. Gold, alert to the treat signal, abandoned Royal and joined me at the counter. I doled out a squishy liver tidbit, peering around for his companion. Miss Copper was nowhere to be seen, which was unusual. The Treat Sound was like a magnet for Her Portly Highness.

"The pills worked like a charm. I'm fine around animals as long as I take one a day." He closed the fridge. "You don't have much food."

"Yes, I do. I have leftovers. Vaughan keeps me supplied."

Royal leaned against the counter. "I was going to make breakfast."

"I have cereal. And there's bread in the freezer." I made a move toward the cupboard but Royal shook his head. "What, you don't like cereal?" I went to the fridge and pulled open the bottom freezer. "I think there's some bacon here. And I have eggs."

"That's a start," he conceded. He took the bag of bacon pieces I handed him. "This isn't bacon."

"Bacon is messy. Crumbles are easier."

"What can you use crumbles for?"

"I sprinkle them on bread for a BLT, I toss them in salad, I—"

"I get the idea." He frowned at my cupboards. "Do you have a skillet?"

I tapped the drawer under the stove with one toe. "I usually have a slice of toast and that's it. I don't do much cooking."

"I usually have more. And I do a lot of cooking." Royal rummaged in the drawer, finally pulling out my Teflon-coated fry pan. He wiggled it. "This is toxic, you know."

"It's also easy to clean. And I don't use it much."

"Obviously. They changed the forecast." He nodded toward the living room. "Snowstorm starting this afternoon into tonight."

"What?" I went into the living room where Miss Copper was curled into the blanket that was formed into a little cat nest on the couch. She regarded me with sleepy gold eyes, stretched, yawned, and resumed napping. Her sleeping arrangements apparently trumped the treats.

I stared at the TV, tuned to the local news channel, the volume low. I cranked it up in time to hear the weatherman say, "…the path has shifted, so we'll be bruised by this one. We thought it would stay north, but it may just dip farther south than we thought."

"Damn," I muttered. "We're supposed to go to a football game tonight."

"It's canceled," Royal called from the kitchen. "Check the closings at the bottom of the screen."

Sure enough, there was ticker-tape-like string of school and event closings ambling along the screen's edge. I went back to the kitchen to lean against the doorway and watch Royal poke through my kitchen cupboards.

"Did you sleep okay?" he asked.

"Kind of. How about you?"

"Your cat snores."

"Did he sleep with you?" I regarded Mr. Gold, who was in the classic Cat Loaf position on the floor at the edge of the counterspace. That way he could keep an eye on Royal and any potential food that might come his way.

"He slept. Me, not so much. The other one came in. They pretty much took over the bottom part of the couch. They're warm, that's for sure."

"Sorry. I thought they'd avoid you. They usually sleep with me."

"Don't worry about it. It won't be the first time I lost some sleep."

I suddenly realized I looked like crap. I had bed head, baggy sweats, and I wore a wrinkled flannel shirt two sizes too big. Royal, on the other hand, appeared good for a guy who spent the night on the couch. His cheeks had gray-and-white stubble and his hair was a bit disarrayed but otherwise he was none the worse for wear. He wasn't wearing the sweater from last night, just a gray shirt with rolled-up sleeves. I spied a bit of white T-shirt at the neck of the shirt.

"I made coffee."

I jerked my attention away from his attire. Why was I staring at him? I mean, granted, the black jeans and gray shirt were great with his white hair and the stubble on his cheeks, but that didn't mean...

"When was the last time you cleaned your coffee maker?"

I considered the question. "You mean the vinegar bath stuff?" Royal nodded. I thought about it.

"Never mind. If you don't remember, it's probably been a while." He opened a drawer, staring inside. "Is everything okay? Are you okay?"

"Yeah, sure. Great." I headed for the kitchen. "A serial killer is after me, and there's a snowstorm on the way. Why wouldn't things be great?"

Royal stilled, his hand poised in mid-air near a door handle. "The snowstorm complicates things." He pulled a couple of plates out of the cupboard. "I thought I'd make scrambled eggs. Do you have a mixing bowl?"

I pointed to the drawer near the sink.

"Do you have any bowls that aren't metal?"

"Nope."

"Hmm."

"What's wrong with metal mixing bowls?"

"They're fine for making whipped cream, but I prefer glass when I'm cooking or baking."

I tugged at my hair, loosening it from its haphazard braid. "I don't bake."

"I sort of guessed that." He took out a metal mixing bowl and proceeded to crack eggs into it. "Do you have any herbs or spices?"

"Vaughan gave me a spice rack thing for my birthday last summer." I opened the cupboard nearest me and pulled out the circular gadget. "See, all kinds of stuff."

Royal finished cracking eggs and inspected the selection, spinning the carousel of small shakers. "I wonder how old these are."

"Like I said, I got it last summer."

"And how long did it sit in the store?" He selected four or five of the shakers and went back to the mixing bowl.

"I suppose you only use fresh stuff."

"I grow my own herbs. That's the only way to be sure you're getting a quality product."

"How do you grow herbs if you have an apartment?"

He shook something green into the eggs. "Come over sometime and I'll show you. I think you might be surprised what can be grown indoors." He shook in a few more things, sniffing suspiciously at one of the shakers and setting it aside.

"What did you mean about the snowstorm complicating things?"

"What did you have planned for today?"

I raked my hands through my hair, working out the

night tangles. "I need to get groceries for tomorrow night's barbeque. I want to finish a sculpture I'm working on and put the finishing touches on a painting I'm doing for Vaughan's birthday. Then I was going to meet the guys tonight for the football game." I jerked my thumb over my shoulder. "Which I guess is now canceled."

"You're going to barbeque?" Royal stared out the kitchen window. "In a snowstorm?"

"It'll quit snowing by tomorrow. My grill is under a cover out on the deck. All I have to do is shovel a path to it." I went to the coffee maker and poured myself a mug of coffee. "I do need to go to the store and get some supplies, though."

Royal whipped the eggs in the bowl, holding it nestled against his side while he beat at it with a fork. "I talked to my office. I'll drive you to a coffee shop. You're going to meet a friend there. She'll spend the rest of the day with you while you shop and do whatever. Then she'll drop you at Deputy Sterling's house for dinner tonight since the game has been canceled. You'll be staying there tonight."

"Did you talk to Finn already today? What friend?"

"Yes, Deputy Sterling and I have been in touch. Your friend happens to be a sheriff's deputy in the next county on loan to this county while we're hunting Mann."

Hunting. There it was again, that reminder. It was so unreal. I was standing here in my kitchen, chatting with a cop about how a madman was going to try to kill me. Meanwhile, the world outside seemed the same as it did the night before. Shouldn't things be different? There was a seismic shift in my life. Why wasn't it apparent in the world?

Nothing made sense.

"He'll make his move today, won't he?"

Royal put down the bowl and put a generous dab of butter into the frying pan which sat on the stove on a burner over a low flame. "Like I said, the snowstorm may complicate things. We think he planned his other attacks very carefully, taking his victims at a pre-determined place and time. If he made plans about you, they'll be messed up now because of the snowstorm." He slid the beaten eggs into the skillet and took a wooden spoon from the drawer next to the stove. "Why don't you start some toast?"

I pulled half a loaf of bread out of the freezer and popped three slices into the toaster. Then I rooted around in the fridge and found the jar of strawberry jam. I took it and some knives and forks to the small table in the corner of the kitchen, then I joined Royal at the stove. "Why didn't you put in any bacon?"

"I'm going to. It'll toughen the eggs if the fats dissolve while the eggs are cooking." He stirred the eggs hypnotically slow, with a measured, precise movement. "It's better to get them going first then add the fats."

"How do you know so much about cooking?"

"I like to read cookbooks." He put down the spoon and rifled through the utensil drawer, pulling out a whisk.

I wrinkled my nose. "What is there to read in a cookbook?"

"Some of them are surprisingly interesting." He whisked the eggs in the pan, beating them vigorously. "*The Joy of Cooking,* for example, has lots of information about cuts of meat and how different herbs and spices interact with meats at different temperatures. Cooking is just science that tastes good. Or it should taste good." He glanced at me. "I already know you don't read romance novels. What kinds of things do you read?"

"I don't read much," I admitted. "Now and again I read a biography or something fiction. I'm more of a movie kind of person."

"Really? What kinds of movies?" He sprinkled the bacon crumbles into the eggs which also had little green and little red flecks of something that he must have found in my spice rack. The eggs were a lot fluffier than the scrambled eggs I made. I'd have to remember the whisk trick.

"Superheroes. Shoot-em-ups. Sci-fi."

He whisked again, fluffing it all around in the pan, the heat so low the gas flame was barely visible. "DC or Marvel?"

"You're getting personal, now."

"How about that?" He tilted his head to regard me. One curly lock of hair bounced onto his forehead. I resisted my impulse to touch it. "You heard me. DC or Marvel?"

"There's Iron Man and Cap America and Thor on the one side."

"And Batman and Superman and Wonder Woman on the other side. Get the plates, would you?"

I picked up the plates from the counter. "I guess I'm just a DC girl at heart."

"Nobody's perfect." He turned off the heat and slid a third of the eggs onto one plate and the rest onto another. "Get the toast."

I put the slices onto a plate and went to the table. "You sit back there." Royal nodded to the seat tucked into the corner. He took the seat in front of the window and the plate with the larger portion.

"Aren't you worried that—" I eyed the window and the café curtain that covered the lower half. "You know."

"Sniper?" He shook his head. "The only kill shot to this house is in the living room. The rest of the windows have a bad line of sight." He leaned over to peer through the doorway into the living room. "You're protected back in the corner because you can't be seen from there. But your shop is out for now. The windows in the back are too exposed. So I'm afraid you'll have to wait to finish your painting and your sculpture."

I sat back in the chair, eggs forgotten. "What?"

"We scoped it out."

"We?"

"Deputy Sterling and I discussed it. Eat your eggs before they get cold." He buttered a slice of toast and smeared it with jam then he dug into the eggs with gusto.

I took a bite of eggs, but I didn't really taste it. Kill shot, line of sight. What a different world he lived in. I took another bite, and this time I noticed it. "This is really good. It's so light. My eggs never come out this fluffy."

"It's all in the wrist."

We ate in silence for a minute. I slipped a bit to Mr. Gold, sitting patiently at my feet. "Where did you learn to cook?"

"Here and there. Like I said, cooking is science. I think I have a scientific mind. You, on the other hand, have a creative mind."

"Says the man who sings and acts in plays." I still couldn't get over the casual mention of a kill shot. That reminded me. "You said that Sporty was strangled. Did he—" I toyed with the last of my eggs, slipping another bite to the beseeching critter near me. "Was she—" I couldn't bear to say the words.

"He didn't rape her. He's not capable of that anymore. That's what the doctors say." Royal took a sip of coffee. "He strangled her with one of those stretchy bands you use in physical therapy. Those big rubber band things. Either he did it or someone with him did it. We're not sure how much strength he has anymore. He's dying."

I leaned back, my throat convulsing. "Did she know—was she conscious or was she—was Nimble alive? Did he know what was happening?"

Royal put his hand over mine. "Is it important for you to know that? Do you think it will help you face what's ahead?"

I nodded mutely. I don't think I could speak even if I knew what to say.

"She was drugged. We think she was semi-conscious when he did it. Knowing how he's worked in the past I think he would want her to know it was him. Brian was probably unconscious. We think that Mann worked on him first so Paulina could see what was happening. He was beaten with a baseball bat. The doctors don't think he'll ever regain consciousness. He's on life support right now."

The tears I had been fighting to hold back rolled down my face. I stared at the doorway and the world beyond the windows in the living room, but I didn't really see anything. All I could do was imagine her horror, her fear. Sporty had been one of the feistiest, most confident women I knew. She was energetic and bouncy and so full of life. The thought of Brian, beaten and defeated, was more than I could imagine. Tall, handsome, physically active Brian.

Royal pushed the plates aside and leaned over, taking both my hands in his. "You will be safe, Snow. We're going to get this guy. You'll be with police protection from now until he's caught or until he's killed, whichever happens."

"What if it takes weeks or months?" I shook my head, tears dribbling off my chin. "I can't live with this for weeks. What if he tortures me and makes me wait for him to kill me? I'm not like you. I can't do this. I can't think like a killer."

Royal's hands tightened on mine. "You don't have to do this. I'm doing it for you. Deputy Sterling is doing it. All of the police assigned to this case are doing it." He pushed my hair back over my shoulder, his hand lingering on the side of my face. "You just have to be you. We'll take care of you. I'll take care of you."

I wanted to believe him, so bad. I wanted to pretend that everything would be okay. I eased my hands away from him and wiped my tears with a napkin. "I guess I just have to deal with it. I've never been good at giving up control to anybody. Nobody's ever taken care of me since I was a kid. Even then, my dad and I sort of took turns taking care of each other after my mom died."

Royal put a hand on my shoulder and gave me a little shake. "Let us manage this. It's what we do. You do what you do—live your life." He picked up his coffee mug. "What kind of painting are you doing for your friend?"

I was grateful for the diversion. "It's from a photograph he took when he and Finn were on vacation. It's a landscape scene." I smiled shakily. "I'm not much with portraits, but I'm okay with landscapes. There's a part of it that bugs me. I don't think I have the right colors layered in. I always let projects sit for a bit then come back to them. Usually whatever is bugging me jumps right out."

"You'll have plenty of time to finish it," Royal said. "I'd rather you didn't work on it today, though. For today, stick with public places. We have a list of stores and restaurants we'll have covered. You're just spending a casual day out with a friend, but you'll be watched the whole time. We already adjusted the schedule when the weather changed. You'll have dinner with Deputy Sterling and stay overnight at his house because of the weather."

My landline phone rang. I inched past Royal to go to the phone in the hallway near the front door. The display told me who it was. "What does the Evil Queen want at this hour of the morning?" I picked up. "Hello, Aurora. Good morning."

"Why didn't you tell me your friend was killed?" she demanded.

I held out the phone, staring at it as if it had grown teeth and was biting. "What?" I put the receiver back to my ear.

"Your friend called this morning about her death. He thought your father would want to know. Of course he'd want to know, but you should have told me first."

"I don't know what you're talking about." I

wandered to the kitchen, where Royal was busy cleaning off the plates and heading for my dishwasher. Lord knows what he'd think of that poor old ancient machine. "Hey," I hissed. "I never use it. Just do the dishes in the sink."

He looked at the dishwasher then at me. "Why not?"

"You didn't know your friend in Florida was killed? The one your father called Sporty?"

"Hang on a second." I gestured toward the sink. "The dishwasher kind of leaks a bit so I don't use it. I haven't gotten around to getting it fixed."

"Is someone with you?"

"I'm kind of busy." I managed to keep my voice level. "I knew Sporty died. I didn't know that anyone called Roy about it. I was going to tell him myself later." After all this crap is over with and I have a minute to think straight, I wanted to scream.

"It upset him a great deal."

If you think that would upset him, imagine how he'd feel to think a serial killer was after his daughter, hoping to rape or murder her. I bit my lip lest the words leak out. "I'm sure it did," I managed to mumble.

"He has a lot of affection for you and your friends. It was a shock to him."

"It was a shock to all of us," I snapped, my patience fraying. "I'm sorry he was upset, but we're all fucking upset, okay?"

"That's the first time I've ever heard you swear," Aurora said, her voice strained. "I mean, really swear, not fake swear."

"Get used to it." I slammed the phone down. Royal raised an eyebrow. "Don't you start with me," I warned.

He held up his hands. "Wouldn't dream of it."

"I'm going to slap that woman into the next county the next time I see her."

"I'd pay good money to see that."

I took two long steps and glared up into his face. "Stick with me and you will."

"Promises, promises," he murmured. One corner of his mouth twitched.

"Stop it."

"Stop what?"

"That."

"What?"

"You're smiling."

"I am not."

"You are, too."

"Am not."

I threw up my hands. "I can't argue with you."

"Good. I don't enjoy arguing."

I was standing way too close to him. If I leaned forward just a bit, we would be chest to chest, thigh to thigh. His eyes were intent on me, so deep green it was like being among the trees in springtime.

I jerked my gaze away. "I'm going to get changed." I whirled, prepared to stomp out of the room.

"You know, maybe you're not giving your stepmother enough credit. Perhaps she really does worry about your father." I turned on him, prepared to give him a good piece of my mind, but he kept talking, not giving me the chance. "She's married to a much older man. That's probably a worry to her. Maybe he has health issues that she's helping him handle."

The only health issues were probably ones she caused. I didn't say it. I knew Royal wouldn't believe me. He was a typical guy, seeing a pretty woman saddled with an old-man husband and being sympathetic to her. "Maybe," I said. "What time are we meeting the deputy person?"

"Nine o'clock. You've got plenty of time." He took a step toward me. "We'll keep you safe. You'll have round-the-clock protection until we get this guy. He's not going to get to you."

I didn't have any answer for that. I had a terrible, sinking feeling that Royal was wrong, but I couldn't say why I felt it.

I went into the bathroom and showered. I decided to forego hairstyling since I'd probably have hat-head by the end of the day. I considered my wardrobe, not sure how to dress for a day involving a snowstorm and God knows what else. I settled on black jeans, a warm red sweater over a white turtleneck, and my sturdy black boots. I dug out my black winter coat with flannel lining from the closet and a wide red headband that served double duty as ear coverings.

A little over an hour later, Royal and I were driving into town in his SUV. We drove to the local grocery store where Deputy Wilma Jacobs met us in the parking lot. She hopped out of a small SUV when Royal pulled into the space next to her. She was a short, solid woman with clipped brown hair and a brisk no-nonsense personality.

"I'll see you later tonight." He stood with me in the parking lot. "I'm joining you for dinner."

"Good. Vaughan's cooking will impress you, and so will his kitchen." I turned to go into the store, but Royal put his hand on my arm and pulled me to him.

"You're well taken care of." He kissed me quickly.

"Try not to worry too much."

I saw Jacobs' surprised expression. "You're startling the troops," I murmured.

"They'll cope. Tell you what. When this is over, I'll show you how to make scrambled eggs."

When this is over. I liked the sound of that. "I'll hold you to it." I turned to Deputy Jacobs.

"Wait a minute," he said. "Reciprocity. What are you going to teach me?"

I thought about it. "I'll teach you the Boot Scootin' Boogie."

He smiled. "Deal. See you tonight." Royal got back into his SUV and was gone.

I joined my new best friend. "Now what do we do?"

"Now we spend some money." She led the way into the grocery store with a grin. "What do we need?"

I piloted the shopping cart while she tossed items in. My eyes kept darting around, trying to spy police until she finally said, "You won't see them. At least, you'd better not see them. They're supposed to blend in. Do you want T-bone or ribeye steaks?"

"T-bone," I said. "Get three. And some of those potatoes." I pointed to the twice-baked potatoes in the meat case. "Where are we going after this?"

"The mall." She grinned at my grimace. "Yeah, I feel the same way, but it's a controlled environment and easy to police. We'll hang out there for an hour or so. Then we go back to your place and stow the groceries. Then we eat some lunch and I drive you over to Deputy Sterling's house."

"Aren't you worried about the traveling to and from? What if he tries to run me off the road the way he did the other night?"

"Our people are all around you. They followed you as soon as you left your house. You're in a cocoon of cops."

My mobile phone chimed "Friends in Low Places" from my purse. I pulled it out and saw Nerdy's phone number. "Hey, you. I suppose you saw that the game is canceled."

"Yeah, I did. I'm at my sister's place, out at the farm. It's starting to snow here."

I stood on my tiptoes to get a glimpse out the front window of the store. Low-hanging clouds seemed like they might go liquid at any moment. "Still dry here but not for long."

"Let's forget about tonight and get together tomorrow. I don't want to navigate country roads in the snow."

"That works for me. I'll talk to you tomorrow."

"Hey, did Finn get a line on the hospital? We need to send flowers or something."

He didn't know. Why tell him? Why ruin his night? "I'm seeing him tonight. I'll find out," I lied. "We'll handle it."

"Okay. Talk to you tomorrow." He hung up.

I started to put the phone away then I saw the flashing red *Voicemail* icon. I didn't recognize the phone number. I tapped the icon.

"Miss DeWitt, this is William Grimes. I work at Mercy Med Center in the patient ombudsman office. Your father was brought in. I've been trying to reach you. He's very distraught. His wife is with him, but he's asking for you. She said she wasn't sure how to contact you. We had your number on file here from the time he was admitted with that broken arm. Could you call me as soon as you can?"

Deputy Jacobs came back to the cart with a head of lettuce in her hand. "What's wrong? Is there a problem?"

"I'm not sure." I tapped the man's phone number, and it rang. I was almost ready to give up when someone answered. "Grimes here."

"This is Natalie DeWitt. You called me earlier about my father?"

"I'm so glad I got in touch with you. Your father was admitted to Mercy Med Center today, and he'd like to see you. Can you come?"

I thought immediately of Roy's previous car accident or accidents. "Of course, I can. Change in plans," I murmured to Jacobs. "What's wrong with him? Was it an accident?"

There was a pause. "We're not quite sure. He's acutely ill. It might be food poisoning or—we're waiting for test results to come back. He's been transferred to a room from the Emergency Room. Please check in at the front desk for his room number. We may need to transfer him to Intensive Care. His condition is quite serious."

Chapter 11

I explained the situation to Deputy Jacobs. "I have to get to the Med Center." I pushed away the full grocery cart. "I can't haul around all this food. I have to—"

"You need to take a deep breath." Jacobs made a beeline for the front of the store. "The first thing to do is verify that this isn't a hoax. I'll make some calls while we get checked out. If it's valid, I'll take you to the hospital. We'll have somebody take this stuff to your house, feed your cats, and make sure things are okay there in case you need to stay at the hospital for a time." She pulled out her phone while she pushed the cart, deftly dodging slower shoppers.

I took over the cart from her, and she flashed me a grateful smile. I was happy to have something to occupy me. What was Aurora doing, saying she couldn't get in touch with me? She had my mobile number. I checked the recent call list and my text messages, but there was nothing from her there.

A checkout lane opened miraculously when we approached. I angled my cart in and dug in my purse for my credit card. The checker and bagger were fast as lightning, and we were done in record time. "Need help with these sacks?" the bagger, a burly young man, asked.

"Sure." Jacobs brushed past me, phone in hand.

The man walked with her to the door, with me trailing behind. "What's the status?" he asked in a quiet, conversational tone of voice. "Word came through there's a change in plans."

"We need to go to the Med Center downtown. The client's father was admitted today. I verified, and it's legit. S.A. Royal is coordinating new security there." Jacobs smiled and nodded while she spoke, just like anybody making pleasant conversation with a grocery store worker.

For his part, the guy—or cop or whoever he was— leaned on the cart just like any checkout guy, not going too fast or slow so we could easily keep pace with him. "That might be tricky. Hospitals have a lot of people coming and going."

"Royal is good at what he does," Jacobs said. "He'll get it set up." She smiled knowingly at me. "He's not letting anything happen to our client."

Well, that was encouraging. I stood by the SUV while the guy loaded the bags into the hatch. He slammed it shut and nodded to me. "See you at the hospital," he said with a cocky grin. "I guess I'm working a short shift here today."

Jacobs went to the driver's side, and I got into the passenger side. As I did, I twisted around, trying to spot our escorts. "Stop it," Jacobs said. "They're here. Don't think about them."

I buckled up. "Do you know Royal? I mean, besides this time? Have you worked with him before?"

"Royal? That's what you call him?"

I nodded. "He just never seemed like a Brendan to me. Is this going to screw up your planning? You guys had everything mapped out."

"I meant what I said. He is good. I've worked with him before. He knows what he's doing. This might work to our advantage. He'll see if we can get your father shifted to a special ward, like a quarantine ward. That'll make it easier for us to set up security. If your father is put into Intensive Care, there's usually security there, too, so more security won't seem out of place. The perp is probably scrambling right now, trying to figure out how to make this work. He's at a disadvantage, too. He's probably already reviewed most of the places where you'll go. The hospital is a curve ball that he won't be expecting. It might throw him off his game."

Curve ball. Throw him off his game. That reminded me of Finn and Nimble, both baseball players. And Brainy, who played softball. I stared out the window, my eyes hot with tears when I remembered that beautiful spring so many years ago.

"You're handling this really good," Jacobs said. "It has to be one hell of a shock."

"Shock?" I drew in a long, shuddering breath, trying to force my fear and grief to the background. "Yesterday I was nobody. Today I'm the target of a killer. I can't—I can't grasp it somehow. I'm just going through the motions, trying to make it look good. If I had my choice, I'd go into a room somewhere and scream my head off. Then I'd probably take a golf club and take a swing at somebody."

She was silent for a moment then she asked, "Driver or an iron?"

I turned to her. She was staring straight ahead but I thought I saw the hint of a smile. "Driver," I said immediately. "It gives me longer reach."

She nodded. "Makes sense. There's also a bigger club head so you'd have a bigger point of impact. Yep, makes sense."

"You could drive a little faster," I suggested.

She checked the rear-view mirror. "I want to make sure our guys stay in sight."

"Good thinking." I resumed staring out my window, my crazy thoughts bouncing from one place to another. I kept coming back to the same question—why wouldn't Aurora call me?

We got to the hospital and parked in a security spot on the ground floor of the garage attached to the seven-story building. "Wait here," Jacobs said, getting out of the car.

"But I need to—" I was talking to a door. A man came out of the hospital doorway nearby, and they conferred briefly.

Jacobs walked back to the car. "Let's go." She held my door open and escorted me into the building, where I was met by two men in blue hospital scrubs.

"We had your father transferred to a private room on the fourth floor. There are only a few other people in rooms on that floor. Most of them are on the opposite side of the floor. He's near the nurse's station. We'll have people positioned there around the clock. No one can go in the room or out of it without being checked." Jacobs spoke while we walked, one man ahead of us and one behind.

"Who are they?" I nodded at the man ahead of us.

He turned slightly and lifted his shirt. I saw a badge of some kind clipped to the waistband of his bottoms along with a small black rectangle, like a pager. "Feds?" I asked Jacobs.

"Local P.D." She pulled out her phone and checked the display. "Your father's doctor will meet us at his room. He's being paged now." We got to an elevator, and she gestured me inside. The two men got in after us, and we rode in silence to the fourth floor. I tried to examine them surreptitiously. If they were armed, where were their guns? They'd be armed, wouldn't they? Granted, the scrubs were baggy, but they couldn't hide a holster, could they?

I watched Jacobs when we left the elevator and began a maze-like journey through hallways. She must be carrying a gun, too, but where? She did have on a loose sort of sweater, so maybe that hid the holster at her waist. But then I saw her move and the sweater shifted and no holster was visible.

We entered a hospital corridor with doors to patient rooms on each side. Roy's room was on the right side, across from a large U-shaped desk with computers and monitors on it. I spied Aurora talking to a short, bald Black man in a white hospital jacket. I wondered if she'd just rolled out of bed. She wore no makeup, and her hair was bundled up on her head in a haphazard ponytail. Her clothing was as haphazard as her hairstyle, faded jeans and one of Roy's old Prince's sweatshirts, stained and frayed.

I hurried to them. "What's going on? Where's Roy?"

Aurora turned. "They told me they called you." She sounded peeved, like I was a big inconvenience or something.

"I'm glad they did," I snapped. I turned to the man. "I'm Natalie DeWitt, Roy's daughter. How he is? What happened?"

"I'm Dr. Winters. I've been treating Roy for the last two years. He's in stable condition. I don't think there will be any lasting damage."

"Two years?" I glared at Aurora, but she didn't meet my gaze. "Damage from what?"

Winters moved away from the nurses' desk, and I followed, Aurora trailing behind us. Jacobs and the other cops fanned out, staying near to me but giving us some privacy. "It appears to be food poisoning. That's what it sounds like, at least, from what Aurora said about the onset of symptoms. We're still waiting on the toxicology reports. We've flushed his system and gave him some medication to settle him. I'd like to keep him in the hospital tonight so we can monitor his recovery, but he should be able to go home tomorrow." He regarded Aurora, his plain face reflecting his sympathy. "How bad has it gotten?"

"I can still manage," she said quickly. "It's not bad."

He considered her then he turned to me. "I'd like to have a conference after you've seen your father. I think you and Aurora and I need to discuss your father's care."

"No, we're fine," Aurora protested. "There's nothing to—"

"Thank you," I said firmly. "I'd appreciate a chance to talk." I ignored Aurora's exasperated sigh. "Can I see him now?"

"He's resting, but yes, you can go in. Just stop at the nurse's station when you're done and have someone page me. We'll talk about his future care." He nodded to Aurora then he left, hurrying down the hall.

"You shouldn't get involved," Aurora said. "Your

father doesn't want—"

"I don't care what he wants," I interrupted. "I am involved, and that's final." I pushed open the door and went into the room.

I didn't see Roy at first. He blended in with the bed, which was on my right, not far from a window that faced the parking lot. Roy's hospital gown was a pale blue, and the blankets were pale blue, too. The head of the bed was raised slightly, and his skin was almost as pale as his white hair. A tube attached to an IV drip was hooked into one skinny arm. An oxygen gadget was clamped on his finger, hooked up to a monitor on wheels next to the bed. A nurse stood on the other side of the bed from the doorway, talking to him. "...quiet, Mr. DeWitt. You need to let the medicine do its work."

"I told you I don't want to be here," Roy said, his voice wheezy and harsh. "I want to find my daughter and make sure she's okay. I'm worried about her."

"I'm just fine, as you can see for yourself," I said, going to his side. "You silly guy, what are you doing, scaring us all like this?" I leaned over and kissed his cheek, trying to avoid the tubing and wires.

"Thank God you're here, Princess. I was so worried about you after that phone call this morning. I don't know why they brought me here. It's just a touch of the flu. There's no reason for all this crap." He flailed out his right arm, gesturing to the tubes and clamps attached to his left arm. "I think she's behind it. She gave me those pills to take, and that's what made me sick. It's her fault." He nodded, his white hair fluttering around his forehead like gauzy agitated birds.

"It's okay, Daddy." I managed to grab his hand and squeezed it. "I'm here. I'll make sure you get the right treatment. You just rest and get your strength back." I smiled at him, and he smiled tremulously in return.

"Well, as long as you're okay, then I can rest." He pushed back on the bed, sighing. "I am tired. All that puking wore me out."

I wrinkled my nose. "I'm sure it did. You sleep now. When you wake up, we'll figure out the best way to get you home."

"Okay," he mumbled, his eyes fluttering closed. "You take care of things, Princess."

I patted his hand and pulled away from the bed. The nurse followed me to the door. "I'm so glad you came," she said softly. "He was so agitated. We just couldn't get him to calm down."

I paused in the doorway to look back at Roy. He was almost asleep, a faint smile on his face. "I didn't know he was sick."

"It happens with dementia patients," the nurse said sympathetically. "They frequently have these bouts of agitation followed by calmness. I know how bad it's been for his wife." She left the room, leaving me staring after her in astonishment.

Dementia? Roy? He was only in his mid-seventies. There was no history of dementia in our family. What was she talking about? I left the room, crossing the hall to join Aurora at the nurse's station. "Why didn't you tell me?" I demanded. "What's been going on?"

Aurora moved away from me. I snagged her arm, jerking her to a halt. "He said you gave him pills to take. Is that true? Did you deliberately—" I hesitated. Poison was such a horrible word. "Did you deliberately make him ill?"

She shrank back. "I would never do that. I always

keep the medication locked. He got sick after breakfast. We ate early because that phone call woke him up."

"What call?" I leaned closer to her. "What did you do?"

Jacobs interposed herself between us. "The doctor said he wanted to talk to you. Your father is stable now, and he needs to rest. You guys need to figure out what's next." She leaned over the counter and spoke to the nurse there. The nurse nodded and pointed down the hall. "Come on. The doctor will see you in one of those conference rooms." Jacobs started walking away from Roy's room, heading for one of the two guys in scrubs who now stood outside a door that was four or five doors away from Roy's.

I followed her, not waiting to see if Aurora joined us. I got to the room, and Jacobs went inside, checking that it was empty. She came out and nodded. "One of us will be outside here. Take your time. Give me your coat. I'll put it in your father's room."

I shrugged out of my winter coat and handed it and my headband to her, then I went in. It was a nondescript room, like the kind surgeons use when they consult with a patient's family. Bland pictures on the wall, two love seats and two armchairs in a soothing, neutral pattern, and magazines on the faux wood end table. I took a seat in an armchair. Dr. Winters came in behind me, going to the love seat opposite me. After a few seconds Aurora came in and took the seat next to me.

"Roy's condition is stable, and he'll recover from this," Winters said without preamble. "But I think we all know you can't care for him at home anymore, Aurora. You were barely able to control him this time."

"Control him?" I turned to Aurora, but she refused

to look at me. "What does that mean?"

"Roy has progressive dementia," Winters said gently. "It's caused by deterioration of brain tissue, which was caused by the chemicals he used in his business, decades ago. There are well-documented cases of this occurring. There were very few safety standards in place years ago. Field workers and people in the landscape trades were often exposed to some extremely dangerous chemicals."

I leaned back in the chair. "I had no idea. He never said anything to me."

"He didn't want you to know." Winters kept his eyes on Aurora, but she didn't volunteer any information. "He has good days and bad days, but lately he's had a lot of bad days, hasn't he?"

Aurora nodded mutely.

"He has difficulty recognizing old friends and old locations. He's having paranoid periods where he's afraid of the people around him. We have him on a rather low dose of medication to keep him stabilized, but it's only going to progress and cause more problems. Aurora, you can't watch him constantly. You need to have home health care. You need to start planning for the future."

"He doesn't want to go into a nursing home." Aurora's head was still lowered, and her voice cracked when she spoke.

"I realize that, but you ladies need to discuss his care," Dr. Winters said. "His health probably won't improve. He'll have more and more episodes like this one."

I stared at Aurora, but she merely nodded, as though it wasn't a surprise to her. I started to ask her about it then Winters said, "I realize you're accustomed to such behavior, Aurora, but you can't continue to care for him at home. As we discussed before, there's an excellent facility on the south side of town. We can get him on the waiting list there. I can make some calls. We can see about getting him in there temporarily so you can make sure it works for him."

"You've talked about this before?" I sat back, stunned. "How long have you known about this?"

Winters stood. "I know Roy didn't want his daughter involved, but it's only fair that she be kept in the know on the decisions being made. The nurse told me how he reacted when she was with him. Bringing her in the discussions might help ease his worry."

"What's going on?" I demanded. "What discussions? What worry?"

Winters walked to the door. "You can use this room as long as you need. Have the nurse contact me when you're done. We'll discuss how to proceed."

"Proceed with what?" I twisted in the chair to watch him.

"Talk it over with your father's wife. Then we'll talk." He left the room, pulling the door closed behind him.

I turned to Aurora. She appeared miserable, staring down at her clasped hands, her eyes red-rimmed and her face all blotchy. "Tell me what's happening. What did you do to him?"

"It wasn't me." Her voice was different than I'd ever heard before. She sounded old and defeated, not the usual bouncy, effervescent trophy wife I'd come to know and hate. "Roy has been getting more and more confused lately. It's because of the chemicals."

"But that was so long ago." I was trying to make sense of it all. "A long time ago."

She raised her head and faced me, her usually smooth and flawless face distorted by grief. "Roy and I have been living a lie. It's time you know about it. He was so afraid that if you knew about it, you'd love him less. I told him that wouldn't happen, but he was so frightened, so worried."

Fear and misgiving overcame my anger. "Tell me," I said, trying to sound gentle and not too insistent. "What's been going on?"

"It started five years ago." Aurora reached into the designer purse at her feet and pulled out a hankie. "I was married then to a real bastard of a man. He owned that industrial park out west of town. You know the one. It's where your father's company did that big landscaping job five years ago. We had a house in the suburbs. Your father did the landscaping there, too."

I nodded my understanding while she dabbed at her eyes and nose. "I remember Roy talking about that industrial park job. He said the client was a pain to work with."

"That was my husband." Aurora's voice sounded raw, like the words hurt to say. "I met him when I was younger and I was in a bad spot." She raised her head, her eyes haunted. "I can't talk about that. I'll just say that he seemed like a prince, there to rescue me. He took care of me, and he bought me clothes, and he showed me how normal people lived. When he said he wanted to marry me, I thought I was set for life."

She fell silent. I resisted the urge to shake the truth out of her. I could tell this was a relief to her, this unburdening of her past. I tried to respect that. "When did it go bad?"

"Almost immediately. He hurt me when we had sex. He liked it that way. I tried to say no, but he told me I couldn't. I was married to him. He'd bought me, and he could do anything he wanted to me." She twisted the hankie, her gaze fixed on the floor. "That's when I met Roy." She sniffled, dabbing her nose again. "He was supervising the landscaping at our new house. We talked. He had questions about the landscaping and I was there."

She rubbed her forehead. "Roy guessed what was going on. He saw the bruises and some days I couldn't walk good because of—" Aurora fell silent. "Because. Your father told me that I didn't have to put up with it. He said he'd help me."

I could imagine Roy doing that. He had zero tolerance for any kind of bullying. If he saw someone picking on a weaker person, he would step right in. "How could he help?" I prompted.

"My husband had been telling me that he regretted marrying me. 'I should have just kept you as my whore,' he'd say. I didn't fit in with the life he wanted, the country club life he thought he could buy his way into. When he first told me, I was afraid. I didn't have anything. I had no skills and no way to support myself. I begged him to keep me. I let him do anything he wanted because I was afraid to be alone." Aurora hung her head, tears rolling off her face.

"But then you met Roy," I prompted.

She nodded. "He told me he would help me if I got divorced. But I would have to help him, too. We made a deal. The next time my husband threatened me with divorce, I told him to do it. I'd sign the papers. He didn't believe me at first. I think he was disappointed. He wouldn't have his sex toy to play with anymore. But then he thought it over, and he realized a quiet divorce would be the best thing that could happen. He filed the papers. I was left with the clothes he bought me and nothing else. Roy gave me money to get an apartment and helped me get a job at a clothing store. Six months after that, Roy and I were married."

"What was the deal?" I asked.

"Roy knew he was dying. The doctors told him that the materials he used in landscaping decades ago were slowly destroying his brain cells. It took years for it to show up. By the time it did, the damage was done. The best he could hope for was to slow the progression. The damage, combined with aging, meant he would start to lose his functioning."

I leaned back, closing my eyes briefly, as though I could blot out the thought of my active, happy father losing his mind.

"I would be his nurse. That was our deal. I'd care for him. When he died he'd leave me enough money that I could go back to school and learn a trade. I wanted to be a landscaper, like him. He promised me he'd see to it I got into the technical college where I could take classes. He'd make sure I had a job when I got out." Aurora watched me, as though gauging my reaction to his. "He was going to leave you a letter, telling you all about it. He hoped you would hire me for the business."

"Why didn't he tell me?"

"He didn't want you to know. I tried to tell him that he was shortchanging himself and you. I told him that you two needed to spend time together while he could enjoy it, while you could enjoy him. But he didn't want you to see him falling apart."

"You should have told me," I blurted. "No matter what he wanted."

"Maybe." Aurora blew her nose then tucked the hankie back in her purse. "I love him, Snow. I'm not in love with him, but I love him, and I respect him. I did what he wanted. We changed the house so it would be easier for him. Got rid of things that agitated him, like reminders of the past. He's so afraid of losing his dignity, of being less of a man in your eyes. I told him it wouldn't matter to you. I told him you loved him no matter what. But it worried him. It frightened him."

I put my hand over hers where it rested on her chair arm. Guilt warred with remorse and anger and fear and pity. I think sympathy won. "I'm sorry," I said. "I should have known."

"There was no way you could. It's just that—" She closed her eyes briefly and swallowed, hard. "It's gotten bad the last few months. He's fighting me sometimes, about the pills." Her blue eyes were bloodshot and red-rimmed. "I'm not afraid of him hurting me, but he might hurt himself. I'm not sure if I can manage it anymore."

"You don't have to do it alone." I squeezed her hand. "We'll figure out something together. We can get a nurse to come in and help. Or maybe I can come over sometimes. I'm not working anymore, so I have time. Or you can bring him to my house. We'll putter around in the shop or the yard."

Her shoulders sagged with visible relief. "That would be such a help," she whispered. "I can't really leave him alone anymore. There's a support group I like to go to where I can talk to other caregivers like me. And I try to sneak out to the gym now and then, usually when Roy's asleep. Thank God the grocery store delivers right to the house now." She managed a brief smile. "Roy loves their apple pie. You know how he is about apples."

I nodded. Roy would eat apple pie day and night if given the chance.

"I can't stand fruit pies, but I always get him some of those small, individual ones from the grocery. He was so upset today after that call about your friend who died. I thought a slice of pie and a cup of tea might calm him down."

"Who called you?"

She shook her head. "I don't know his name. He's called Roy before. He said he's an old friend of yours from school."

"Probably Vaughan," I murmured. "He and Roy always did get along so well."

"Roy was so upset when that other girl died last year, too. I think he felt like your college friends were his kids." Aurora sighed heavily. "I always worry about him, even though I hide his car keys and lock the kitchen drawers and the medicine cabinets. I'm always afraid he might get into something and hurt himself."

Good God, what a life. I could only imagine her constant worry. "We'll figure something out," I promised.

We both stood. "I'm sorry I didn't tell you sooner." Aurora walked to the door.

"I understand why you didn't." I still blamed her, but I wasn't going to voice it. She had enough guilt as it was.

Aurora opened the door and stepped out into the hallway. "I'll stay with him until I'm sure he's asleep, then I think I'll go home and change." She touched her ratty sweatshirt. "I grabbed the first thing I could find this morning." We walked down the hall to Roy's room. The area was surprisingly quiet. Jacobs had said that there weren't a lot of patients around, so that probably accounted for it.

A man in dark blue hospital scrubs stepped out of Roy's room and spotted us. "Mrs. DeWitt? I'm the new nurse on duty. Can we talk?"

Aurora hurried forward to join him, and they went into Roy's room. I hung back, trying to find Jacobs or one of the guys who were with us earlier. I started toward the nurse's station, but the door to a room on my right flew open. I glimpsed linens and shelves of tissue boxes and water containers. A man stepped out, his red Crocs catching my eye. They were such a startling color in the sterile whiteness of the hospital. He wore scrubs with a pale blue background imprinted with snowmen, Santa Clauses, and reindeers on the shapeless top.

I turned, startled by the sudden movement. Then I saw the body on the floor in the room. It was one of the guys who had escorted us into the building. He was sprawled on the floor. I couldn't figure out his position at first. I thought he was lying on his back but then I realized that he was on his stomach, his head twisted at an odd angle. His eyes were open, and he stared sightlessly at me.

Chapter 12

It took me a second to process what I was seeing. I drew breath to scream, but the guy in the Santa Claus scrubs pressed something against my face. I sucked in a long breath, tasting cloth and inhaling something sweet.

It didn't affect me at first. I pushed at the cloth, trying to escape the man and his arm around my upper chest. I gasped again, and this time I felt it. I couldn't quite figure out where I was. I knew I was in a building. I knew something was wrong. But everything felt cloudy or stupid.

Then I was sitting down. I was moving. I stared straight ahead, but the things I saw didn't register until long after they were past. It was like being in a slow-motion movie or a movie where the sound didn't match up to the mouths. I think there were people around me. I saw things, but the images didn't make it to my brain for processing. I was foggy.

"Ow." Somebody jabbed my arm.

"It'll take full effect in a few minutes." The voice came from above me.

I opened my eyes. All I saw was my lap. My black jeans and my feet. The floor was moving under me. It was a beige linoleum with dark gray flecks. I couldn't tell if I was moving or the floor was. That made no sense, but nothing made sense.

Something bumped me and I tilted, my head lolling

to one side. Noise around me. Dings and a small bell sound. The floor jerked under me. When I focused on it, I saw that it had changed. It wasn't tile now. It was metal or cheap carpet. I tilted my head, trying to figure out where I was. Brown panels surrounded me. Someone was next to me. I saw Santa Claus and a snowman. That was odd. Santa was so close I could see his fat red nose.

I opened my mouth to talk, but I felt like my lips were glued together. When I finally did get them peeled apart, I couldn't form a sound. When I tried, I gurgled. It was like in a dream, when I tried to walk but quicksand held me in place or when I tried to scream but nothing came out. That's what it was. A dream.

Someone's hand landed on my shoulder, squeezing painfully. "Don't try to talk, sweetie. It's all okay." The voice had a faint Southern lilt to it. "She's still feeling those pain killers, I guess. Thank God for them, right?" A person laughed nearby.

I tried to talk again. This was wrong. I should be able to talk. I shouldn't be sitting here. I wasn't sure where I was supposed to be, but it wasn't here. I grunted, forcing the sound out. Cool air washed over me, and the light around me changed. Voices spoke softly. It was too much effort to try to see. I closed my eyes.

When I opened them again, cold air surrounded me. I was still seated but I wasn't moving. Snow was falling. It was a white curtain around me. My legs had a dusting of white, startling on the black of my jeans. Under my booted feet I saw snow, pristine and untouched, but nearby I saw snow with tire tracks.

"...need her coat because it's just a short trip." The

voice came from beside me somewhere. "We won't be out in this…"

Yes, I did want my coat. My sweater was getting damp from the snow swirling around us. A dusty, pungent smell was around me. Dry in the wet air. I struggled to raise my head. There was a vehicle not far away. The smell came from it. *Exhaust fumes.* The words appeared in my brain, but it took a few seconds for me to realize they applied to the vehicle. It was white and not because of the snow. It was painted white. There were doors in back, and they were open.

My vision distorted, tunneling into a narrow point then opening widely. My stomach lurched with each dizzy blink. I focused on a tall pole in the middle of the vehicle. If I focused on it, I wouldn't get sick. I clung to it like a physical entity. Don't focus anywhere else. Look just at that shiny metal pole. Nowhere else. Don't move.

Someone pushed the chair I sat in. I closed my eyes when the world lurched around me. Coldness settled on my hands. The snow was melting. It didn't hurt. It was just cold.

"Natalie! What's going on?"

I knew the voice. It was someone I knew. I let my head fall to one side so I could peer at the man running toward me. I knew him. He was tall and white-haired. Who was he?

Voices around me. "…friend of mine. What's going on? Where are you taking her?"

Answers. I couldn't understand them. "…ill so we're transporting…"

"But she wasn't…"

"Take him."

"What are you…"

Noises. Clattering, slamming doors, voices talking, an engine. Someone moved me or lifted me. It was odd. I was floating, then I was lying down, but I was still moving. My body shifted back and forth. I didn't care. I was secure, I knew that. But it felt odd to not be in control of what was happening.

"…did you give her? She's so pale."

"…she's pale. She's Snow White, remember?"

"Her breathing is…where are you taking…"

I opened my eyes. The man sat across from me, just a few feet away, his knees level with my face. He was worried, his eyebrows drawn together in a frown. It was hard to see him clearly in the half-light that flickered into the place where I lay. He swayed, too, with the movement of the—car? I peered around the space. It was a van of some kind. There were wires and tubes around me, swinging with movement.

When the man moved, only his body moved. His arms were locked in front of him. That was odd. Why didn't his arms move when the—where was I? Ambulance. The word surfaced in my foggy brain. I was in an ambulance. As if that was a door opening, other thoughts bubbled up through the miasma that still gripped me. I was at the hospital. My father. An image of him popped into my mind, lying in the bed. He was poisoned. A woman was with me. She and I went shopping. What happened to the groceries?

The man leaned forward, his face close to mine. His eyes were a brilliant green color, and his hair was thick and white. "Snow, listen to me."

Snow? Was that me? It sounded familiar. It was snowing outside. Maybe that's what he was talking about.

"You probably had a small dose of chloroform or something to slow you down then they gave you a shot. I heard them talking. You'll be fully conscious soon, but you'll be groggy, disoriented. It's important to remember that I'm your friend. That's all I am. I'm just a friend who was with you at the hospital. Can you remember that?" He reached for my hand. That's when I saw that his hands were tied with a black strap of some kind. The strap in turn disappeared between his legs. Maybe it was tied somewhere.

His hand touched mine. It was cold. That reminded me that I was cold, too. I struggled to find my body. I was dressed, but I was covered with only a thin sheet. I glimpsed whiteness outside through the windows at the back of the ambulance. Snow. There was a snowstorm.

I didn't understand. I tried to form the words, but my throat was too dry, too full of gook of some kind. He must have seen my lips move. "I know. It's confusing. I couldn't get a call in before they took me. I did get rid of my wallet, so they don't know who I am. They got my phone and my gun and your purse. I don't know if we can be tracked. We're on our own."

He was so worried. What was his name? I knew him, but I couldn't remember his name. He was a singer, I think. I remembered him singing.

"They'll want you alert, so the longer you can pretend to be confused, the better. Don't worry. My team will find us. It might take some time, but they'll find us. We just have to hang on until they do."

"Hey! Back off!"

The voice came from behind me. The man facing me turned his head to his right. "She seemed sick. I'm just trying to help." He sounded scared, which was weird because he didn't sound scared earlier.

"You heard me. Back off. Get back to your seat."

"Okay, okay. I'm just worried about her, that's all."

"Worry about yourself." Something slammed and rattled. The man leaned back, but he continued to stare at me, his eyes intent on mine.

It's okay. His lips formed the words, but he didn't speak. *It will be okay, Snow.*

I blinked to show I understood, and he smiled.

The vehicle—no, it was an ambulance. I forced myself to repeat that. An ambulance. The ambulance bounced and slid. Snowstorm. Slick streets. I allowed thoughts to drift through my mind, holding onto stray ideas when they passed like jumping on clouds.

The hospital.

My father. Roy. That was his name.

Poison. He was poisoned.

I was with the police. They were going to protect me.

Someone in Santa Claus clothing put his arm around me.

A man lay on the floor in a room.

The ambulance slid again, and voices behind me cursed. "...plows. They'll see our tracks."

The man across from me...Royal. That was his name. Royal leaned to his right. I think he was trying to appear exhausted but maybe he was trying to hear. Someone was in the front of the ambulance. There was a little window, wasn't there? I saw that when they put me in, didn't I?

"...snowing so hard it'll cover the tracks. I'm not

worried…that. I'm worried about him. He's so fucking weak…see it through."

"That'll be fine…me. This whole thing… stupid…the start. We should…just kill them and get…"

That penetrated the fog. Someone wanted to kill me. That's why I was with the police. They were going to protect me. They were going to catch the man when he tried to kill me.

The man. A man. Mann.

I saw Royal. He was staring to his right. I managed to twist on the bed—no, it was a gurney or a cot—I twisted and craned my neck. I glimpsed a windshield. It was dark, and snow battered against us, swirling with the wind.

A headache suddenly lanced into my brain. I whimpered, falling back on the limp pillow. Royal leaned over me. "Are you okay?"

"Hurts." I was able to get that word out. "Head."

He touched my face. "You'll be okay. I promise. Just remember. Act confused. It might be our best chance. They don't know who I am. It'll be okay. Rest now. You need your strength for what's ahead."

That sounded like an excellent idea. I closed my eyes.

I don't know how long it was, but I was colder than before. Then the ambulance stopped so fast that I shifted on the gurney, almost going feet-first into the doors ahead of me. Curses and shouts erupted from in front of us. "Can't see a fucking thing in this…" A heavy door slammed. Frigid, damp air washed in over me.

I turned my head to my left. Royal was gone. It took a second for that fact to register. Where was he? I tried to sit up but, when I did, a wave of dizziness made me almost puke. I choked and lay back down, closing my eyes until the sensation passed.

I tried again, digging in my elbows to prop myself up. I cautiously looked around. Pale light filtered in from the windows. Royal was there, peering out. "I'm not sure where we are. I think it's a construction site." His hands were held out to the side and I saw the strap that held him to the side of the ambulance. "Get ready." He dropped back onto the folding padded seat that jutted out from the ambulance wall opposite me.

I fell back on the bed, closing my eyes again when dizziness threatened. The doors flung open and wet, icy air poured in over me. I squinted through my eyelashes. Two men jumped into the space. One went to Royal and leaned over him, doing something I didn't see. Then Royal was jerked to his feet and dragged out of the ambulance by the strap wrapped around his hands.

The other man picked up my arm. His fingers clamped onto my wrist so tight I thought he might cut off the blood flow. I kept my eyelashes lowered, getting small glimpses of him when he moved around me. His dark hair was matted wetly against his head, and his nose was red with cold. He wore a sweatshirt jacket over hospital clothes.

Royal said to act confused. The fog was lifting in my brain. I needed to believe him. I couldn't quite remember why, but he was helping me. He would get me out of this, whatever this was. I peered groggily at the face above me. "What?" I muttered.

"I told him he gave you too strong a dose. Idiot." The man went to the door and leaned out. "I need some help here. She's still out of it."

"Hang on!" someone shouted back.

The man came back to my side. His eyes flickered over me, assessing me. I knew what he was thinking. His hand touched my face. I struggled not to grimace, not to show I cared. *Act confused. It might be our best chance.* His hand went lower, to my breast. I felt him caress me, his hand squeezing gently as though gauging my reaction.

"Hurts." I let my head drop to the side.

He chuckled. "There's all kinds of hurt, honey," he whispered with a soft lilting accent. "Maybe he'll let us have a go at you before he does you."

"Time to go." The voice came from the open doorway.

The man next to me removed his hand, and the gurney started to move. I clung to the edges when I was wheeled out, slid from the protection of the van into snow that immediately covered me. The man pushed, and someone else outside pulled. I was soon completely out of the ambulance. The gurney jolted hard, once. I realized I was on the ground, the men pushing me through heavy snowfall. I couldn't see anything. The darkness was complete except for small flashes of brightness that hit my face now and then.

Flashlights? I tried to see through the snow and glimpsed what might be small floodlights at irregular intervals along what appeared to be a path of some kind through piles of dirt and oddly shaped hills.

Then we were inside again, but it was cold and wet all around us. We were inside but still outside somehow. There was protection from the snow overhead, but it still swirled around us, around the feet of the men who walked ahead and behind me. This area was better lit by two portable lights set on a pile of debris on either side of the space.

We stopped, and I was pulled off the gurney. I staggered when the men tipped me, forcing me to my feet. I almost fell. I couldn't feel my legs. My body was uncoordinated, like it didn't belong to me. I was able to lift my head, though, and I peered around while I was forced into a chair and my hands were tied behind me.

The area was lit by two portable lights that shone dimly, illuminating an abandoned building. Outside was an overhead light, the kind left on at construction sites to discourage break-ins. Big windows and a doorway were ahead of me. There wasn't any glass in the windows so that explained the cold. The floor was covered with dirt and what I thought was scraps of lumber and papers. A long bench was in front of one window, painted blue.

I sat back, my head swiveling from side to side. It was my store. I knew that bench. I used to put flower arrangements there, along with some of my sculptures and vases and other gift items for sale. That was the front door ahead of me. On my right were the two abandoned floral coolers, sagging on their bases. Behind me would be the storage room and the checkout desk. On my left was—

A man shuffled toward me from the shadows, clinging to an IV pole while he walked. He was so thin I wasn't sure how he stayed upright. I could see the bones of his wrist sticking out of the sleeves of a jacket that hung limply on him. A tube from the IV vanished into the sleeve. The veins in his neck and hands stood out in sharp relief. It was like watching a skeleton move.

He held up my purse. "You really should set a passcode on your phone, Snow. We disabled the location tracker." He turned. I saw Royal in a chair behind me to my left, leaned forward with his head drooping. "You, however, were a bit more security conscious. We left yours at another location. If you cooperate, you'll live long enough to retrieve it."

Royal slowly lifted his head. I drew back when I saw his face. Red, congealing blood made him almost unrecognizable. His mouth was bruised, blood dribbling from his lip. His right eye was puffy and closed. His left ear was twice the normal size. The collar of his gray shirt was stained with blood, and his sweater was wet around his right shoulder. "Where is it?" he croaked.

The man waved a hand. "Somewhere between here and there. As soon as they got moving and discovered it had a passcode, they threw it away." He tossed my purse at my feet. "I'm curious why you were carrying a gun. And why you weren't carrying a wallet."

"It's legal to carry a gun," Royal managed to answer. "And I must have lost my wallet when your thugs got me."

"Thugs." The man smiled, but it was mirthless, more a grimace than a grin. "Yes, well, perhaps they are, but they do have their uses." He continued staggering forward, pushing the IV pole across the dirty, frozen floor. "Do you remember me, Snow?"

Act confused. I felt Royal watching me. "I don't know you." I peered around the remains of my store. "I don't understand any of this."

Something sounded from my purse, lying on the floor. Santa Claus Man scooped it up, pulling out my phone. "That's the third time this guy has called," he said, glaring at the display.

"He's insistent." The thin man gestured, and another man in jeans and a heavy winter coat stepped forward. He went to Royal and put a gun against the side of Royal's head. "Why don't you talk to your caller and allay his worries? I'd rather not have anyone concerned about your absence."

"Don't hurt him." I managed to get the words out around the fear. "Please."

"Cooperate, and we won't."

I stared at Royal. He didn't act frightened. How could he be so calm? He nodded, just a faint shift of his head. Dear God, help me to think. I need to think. What could I do?

Santa Claus Man came forward, my phone in his hand. He pressed it against my face, leaning close to me so his body was near me. I smelled him, sour and sweaty. I pulled away, but he just moved closer, pressing his groin into my shoulder. I swallowed my nausea and fear.

"Snow? Is that you?"

I struggled to recognize the voice. "Yeah, yeah, I'm here."

"Where have you been? We've been looking for you."

"The hospital," I managed to say. Think. Think. This is Vaughan. Think. What can I say to him? How can I tell him? I saw Royal. The man holding the gun was watching me over Royal's head. "Daddy is in the hospital. Daddy is sick."

"Roy's in the hospital?" Vaughan asked.

"Yes. Daddy." I emphasized the name, *Daddy*. "The job is killing him. I guess the land got its revenge on him." I stared ahead of me at the blue bench. "Daddy and Brendan are in the hospital."

There was a pause. "Brendan, too?"

I nodded then realized how stupid that was. "Yes, Brendan. Daddy is sick, and we went to see him."

There was another pause. "Okay. What can I do to help?"

Santa Claus Man pulled the phone away from me and pressed it against his chest. "Wrap it up, bitch." Then he pressed it against my face again.

"Make sure my groceries get put away," I said. "We bought groceries this morning. I got the tarragon."

"Oh. You did? Good. Yeah. Anything else?"

The other man leaned forward, his back pressing into Royal and the gun hard against the back of Royal's head. I got the message. "I have to go. 'Bye."

Santa Claus Man removed the phone and handed it to the thin man, who shut it off. "Perhaps that will satisfy them that you're fine. Or not. I don't care, one way or the other. You'll be dead by the time they find you."

Just hold on until they find us. Didn't Royal say that? "I don't understand."

"I think you do." He moved forward, the IV pole rattling with each step until he stood in front of me. "I'm your old friend, Hunter Mann."

I tried to appear stunned. But what would a confused, stunned person look like? I gave up on acting. "Mann? From college?"

"One and the same." He gestured grandly, his hand taking in his gaunt appearance. "Not quite the handsome young man I'm sure you remember from your youth."

"What happened?" Keep him talking. They'll find us.

He leaned forward until his face was inches from mine. I saw saliva in the corners of his mouth, yellowing teeth, and skin so dry it was flaking. "You happened. You gave them the courage to tell on me."

"Tell on you?" I leaned forward, too, staring him in the eye. It startled him, and he drew back sharply. "You assaulted them."

"They asked for it. You asked for it." He pointed an accusing finger at me, like that skeletal Ghost of Christmas Future handing down a verdict.

My anger cleared out any remaining cobwebs. "Bullshit."

Mann ignored my outrage. He was too focused on his own tragedy. "My life mirrored yours. You went on to a successful career, a happy life, and people who love you. I was gang-raped in prison, but I went on to a successful career. It just isn't one that somebody puts on a resume." He smiled wolfishly. "Parallel paths in different directions."

"It wasn't my fault."

"Really?" His low and controlled voice told me how much effort it took to keep his rage bottled inside. "You were out there in those little golf skirts, flirting with all the boys. Little Miss Perfect with your friends and your rich daddy. You deserved it. You were asking for it."

"Rich daddy? My father worked hard for everything. Every penny went into his business. I was there on a fucking scholarship." I wasn't scared anymore. I was mad. "There is no way in hell I'm letting you blame me for this. You won't hear me apologizing because you had a hard-on for me."

I saw the slap coming. I almost dodged it in time. His open hand slammed against the side of my face instead of my nose. I gasped when pain exploded, amplifying the headache that was already throbbing in my temples.

"Oh, dear." He reached toward me. "Blood on your pretty skin. Are you sure you don't want to apologize?"

I flinched, but he managed to touch me, running his finger along the side of my face. He held it up. Yep, blood. "Eat shit," I snapped.

He clutched the IV pole, veins visible on the back of his hand and in his throat. I saw no remnant of the handsome young man who charmed the girls in college. There was no fragment remaining of the man who did his damnedest to smear my reputation and that of the other girls. This was a hollow, pathetic, twisted shell of a human being.

He regarded me with calm detachment, like a scientist regards a bug. "I'm going to kill you," he said conversationally. "I'm also going to make sure your father dies. I thought that little episode this morning would do the trick. That whore of a wife of his got him to the hospital in time. Next time she won't be so lucky. You won't be there to see it, of course. But he can join you in hell." His dry, cracked lips twisted. "He loves his apple pies, doesn't he?"

"The grocery store." I struggled to clear out the cobwebs. "You poisoned my father. This was all planned. You wanted me at the hospital."

"Of course. It's a lot easier to kidnap someone from a busy location."

Santa Claus man stepped toward Mann, murmuring

something to him. Mann sighed. "Apparently our exit from the hospital did not go unnoticed. I have little concern for my own safety but my thugs, as your friend so aptly called them, do care about theirs." He shuffled over to Royal to stare down at him. Royal tilted his head to stare through his unhurt eye. The two men locked gazes.

"Do you love him?" Mann glanced to his left at me, his gaunt face sallow in the light.

How should I answer that? If Mann wanted to hurt me, then if I said 'yes', they'd kill Royal. But if I said 'no', then maybe they would assume it didn't matter if he died and they'd kill him anyway. How should I answer?

I met Royal's gaze, mutely begging him to tell me what to do. He blinked slowly then his poor bruised mouth tried one of his half-smiles. "Tell the truth," he gasped, his voice raw.

"I don't know," I blurted. "I think I could love him but I'm not sure."

"What a pity." Mann shook his head in mocking sympathy. "I guess you'll never find out, will you?" He gestured to the Santa Claus man. "He can keep you company while you die."

Santa Claus Man stepped away, the gun disappearing somewhere at his back. He went behind me. I struggled to see what he was doing. My hands were suddenly free, but before I could do anything, Santa Claus Man jerked them over my head and kicked my legs out from under me. I swayed, my knees like jelly. My captor pushed me, and I stumbled, almost hitting the floor. He manhandled me by my sweater and kept me upright, pushing and shoving me across the room to the walk-in coolers on the east wall.

"I originally planned to simply tie you up and leave you to freeze to death," Mann said, watching my progress. "I thought that would be appropriate for the Snow Queen. But then I saw these marvelous coffins. I thought how nice it would be for you to be inside, watching someone you love as he died. The snow will eventually cover you both. You'll suffocate, but not before you see him die." He gestured to Royal. Two other men stepped up, picking up Royal's chair and dragging him near the coolers.

I tried to struggle, but I didn't have a chance. The drug they gave me still had me disoriented. Before I knew it, I was shoved into the cooler, which was three feet wide, three deep, and six feet tall. I remembered those measurements from the time when they were installed. I peered up through the glass ceiling of the cooler. Snow covered it completely. The roof must be missing there. I saw my foot skids in the snow in front of the coolers.

The men tipped Royal so he lay in front of me on his side, still tied to the chair by his hands and feet. I glimpsed his face through snow drifting through the opening above us. He didn't react. I couldn't tell if he'd passed out. Was he even still alive?

Mann approached. "This is how I want to remember you." His emaciated face stared at me through the glass. "So pretty. The ice queen. So perfect. So afraid."

I leaned against the door. The glass was cold and so thick. I knew it was futile, but I tried pounding it. My fist just bounced off. There were no interior door handles on coolers like this because no one was supposed to get inside one.

"Suffocation will kill you. Either that or the cold. That might get to you first." He tapped the glass. "You can't break it. It's locked. This will be your coffin." He wiped at the snow on top of the case. "I'm not going to watch because I know it won't be as satisfying as imagining what you're going through. I will stream it, though." He gestured to the mobile phone on a pile of rubbish across the room, its light glowing. "I can watch it over and over again." He stared at me, his face just inches away.

"Let's go," the man with him said.

Mann stood, wavering for an instant. "Good-bye. I'll see you in hell, Snow." He laughed mirthlessly. "Snow in hell. How perfect."

I twisted in my cage to watch them walk away. One of them moved a floodlight, leaving the place dimly lit by the remaining light. The overhead security light filtered through breaks in the roof, adding to the faint illumination.

I slowly sank down until I rested on the bottom of the cooler, my back against one icy glass wall. I reached out to Royal. It was stupid, but I wanted to touch him. I couldn't stand to see the snow covering his face.

The cold settled on me.

Chapter 13

"Snow."

The voice was so soft I thought I imagined it at first.

"Snow."

I leaned forward. It was hard to see anything. When Mann and the others left, they took one of the lights. The other one was about four feet away on my right and angled toward my prison. It cast long shadows over everything. Where was it plugged in? I tried to find the live outlet but there wasn't a cord. It must be battery-operated. The falling snow only added to the disorientation. The light caught and reflected prisms of moisture, giving the whole thing an aura of softness.

Royal's eyes were open. He was pressed against the ground, his face squashed into the rubble, but he was awake. "Don't say anything." He breathed the words, so softly I had to strain to hear because of the glass that separated us. "I don't know how good his camera feed is or if he's watching it. I don't know if it'll pick up my voice. I'm suspect it'll pick up your voice, though. That's something he'd want to hear. Blink if you understand."

I blinked rapidly.

"Can you think of any way to get out of there?"

I inclined my head.

"You can get out?"

I lifted my shoulders then let them sag. Every cooler had a panic button at the bottom of the door, but I had never used mine. The only time I ever got into the cooler completely was once or twice a year when I cleaned it. Then I kept the door propped open. Otherwise I just leaned in to put floral arrangements on the shelves—the glass shelves that had been removed and now lay gathering snow in a pile of rubble on my left.

I vaguely remembered the literature that came with the coolers, probably a decade ago. These had a latch, not a magnetic closure, so the panic button was required by law. The seal was still somewhat good although in the last year they began to leak. I'm sure suffocation was a real possibility. I had no idea how long that might take.

Even if I could tip the cooler over, it wouldn't break. This was special glass built to withstand all kinds of abuse. I had to be careful hitting the panic button. If the cooler tipped and it landed on the front, I'd never get the door open. The weight of the cooler would prevent that. These coolers could be bolted to the wall, but I didn't do that. They had been wedged into a small display area, keeping them in place. I wasn't worried about them overbalancing.

Now all the display shelving that had surrounded them was gone. They stood alone against what used to be the outside wall of the store. They were heavy and solid, but my weight might tip them.

Of course, this could all be a moot point. I had no idea if the panic button would even work. I sat down, my back at the back of the cabinet. I stared at the floor of the cooler, trying not to focus too much, in case anyone was watching. There it was. The button was really a lever, meant to be pressed on with the foot while the door was being pushed. But if I pushed too hard and the lever didn't work, I might tip.

I had to try. Royal had said someone would find us. I didn't know how long I had, either with air or with the temperatures. Mann was right. The cold was starting to affect me. I wasn't wearing a coat. I was soaked with snow when they wheeled me from the ambulance to the store. The snow had melted through the fibers of the sweater until it felt like I was wearing an icy shroud. A bone-deep frost was settling in while I sat there. Adrenaline had kept me from noticing it before, but now I couldn't escape it.

I scooted forward and peeked at Royal, then at the camera facing me. If I did manage to get out, it would be shown on the camera. If they weren't far away, they might come back to see what we were up to. The camera was level with me, about three or four feet off the ground.

But Royal was sprawled on the floor, slightly below the camera level. I nodded at the camera. He closed his eyes, then he gathered himself, twisting his body in a sharp move to his right. Now he lay on his back, not his side. Snow drifted down on him while he lay there, breathing heavily. Pink rivulets of blood dribbled down the side of his face and from his collar to the floor.

He twisted again, landing on his right side. He dug his feet into the rubble, pushing his body, but he didn't go toward the camera. Inch by painful inch, he turned so he was aiming toward the light. I almost said something but then it hit me—if he knocked over the camera, they would know something was amiss. If the light went out, they might attribute it to the weather or a bad battery.

Royal twisted again. Now three feet separated him from the light. If his legs were free, he could have reached it with a kick, but his ankles were bound to the wooden chair. His shoulders bunched and heaved. I could only imagine the pain. It would have been bad if he weren't already wounded. I had no idea what they did to him, but the pink trail was a darker red now.

He began a jerking, snakelike movement, shoving his legs forward then digging in his right elbow, lifting himself, then pushing his upper torso through the dirt and snow. The debris on the floor masked sound but I wasn't sure how much.

I pounded on the glass. "Help!" I yelled. More pounding. I didn't want to yell. I had to control my breathing. How long did I have? How long would it take to suffocate in a slightly leaky old cooler? "Help!"

Royal was almost there. I kept my eyes off him and focused on the camera in case anyone was watching. But would they watch? Weren't they more worried about getting away without anybody knowing what they did? Someone at the hospital had noticed us. They knew we were in trouble. What was it Royal said? *My team will find us.* How could they find us? I tried to give Vaughan a clue, but I had no idea if he understood or if he'd be talking to Finn anytime soon.

"Get ready." Royal's voice was ghostly, coming out of the darkness beneath the lamp.

I leaned back in the cooler, angling my foot at the lever at the base of the door. The light around me wavered then flickered, the beam aiming crazily for the open ceiling then the floor. Then it was black, the only light coming from the security light filtering through the ruined roof. I jammed my foot against the panic button and pushed as hard as I could on the door.

Nothing happened.

I tried again, rapping the button quickly. The heel of my boot caught the lever and slipped off. The cooler tipped precariously, leaning over to the left then landing back on the right with a cracking noise. The cooler tipped again when it settled. I frantically leaned backward, wedging myself into the far back corner.

I sucked in a shaky breath, but I couldn't seem to suck it in deep enough to fill my lungs. Was it panic or incipient suffocation? I couldn't chance it. Royal was hurt. I had to get myself out of this. I took aim at where I thought the lever was and stomped, pushing with all my might at the front of the cooler.

The door slammed open, and I tumbled out head-first onto the floor. I hit with my shoulder, rolled, hit a pile of debris, and came to a stop on my back. I was a foot or two away from the camera, which was still upright on the pile of boards.

I got to my hands and knees and crawled to Royal. He was lying on his back, snow covering his chest. "Are you okay?" I bent over him, brushing snow away from his face.

"They worked me over." Blood trickled from his mouth. I touched his right shoulder where his sweater was wet and gooey. "A broken rib or two. A lot of lacerations. Maybe a dislocated shoulder. We've got to get moving. See if you can untie me."

I carefully tilted the chair to the side, trying to see what bound him. "It's that plastic stuff," I said. "Those zip tie things. I don't know how to undo them."

"See if you can find something. There must be some nails around here or something sharp."

I knew there were nails, but I didn't see how those would help. I got cautiously to my feet. I knew this space, but now there were piles of debris everywhere. Hurry, hurry. Think. This was my store. Think, think. What did I leave behind?

Maybe a better question was what hadn't been destroyed yet? I stumbled to what used to be the back of my store where we kept all kinds of odd and ends. Faint light filtered in through the holes in the roof. The security light outside didn't quite show everything here, but it did illuminate enough.

A pile of timber made the floor an obstacle course, a big jumble of boards and jagged ends of what had been the old workbench. The workbench. Tools. What did we leave behind? I know we left some stuff that was broken or rusted or just so outdated it wasn't worth keeping or transporting. The company buying the property didn't care. It was all going into a landfill.

I lay on the pile of boards, reaching down and praying I didn't get jabbed by a nail sticking out of a piece of siding or a shard of glass from the windows. There. I felt it. That wooden box. I left behind a few things that just weren't worth saving, like the coolers weren't worth saving.

I reached the edge of the wooden box and tugged, dragging it partway to the light. I pawed through it with one hand, feeling around. A hammer. A spackling knife. A paintbrush, stiff with age and disuse.

Scissors.

I pulled them out triumphantly. They were old and

rusted. Someone had left them in the cooler, and they barely moved, much less cut. But they might serve the purpose. I felt around in the box some more and found a pair of pliers. Maybe, just maybe, they would work.

I made my way back to Royal, bumping into piles along the way and adding more bruises to the ones I'd already collected. I knelt beside him, working the scissors between the flesh of his wrist and the thick plastic cord. I sawed at the white plastic, the rusted old blades barely making a dent. But they made enough of a dent for me to wedge the pliers in there. I leveraged all my strength on the pliers and with one loud snap the plastic broke free.

"Help me up." Royal put his arms on the pile of lumber where the lamp had been sitting, hoisting himself and the chair upright. I steadied him, getting the chair underneath his still-bound legs. I handed him the pliers and I used the scissors. Between the two of us, we got his legs free fast.

He got to his feet and almost toppled over. I put an arm around his waist, drawing his left arm over my shoulders. "Get the phone." He stumbled toward the smartphone that was still recording. I helped him walk, snatching the phone and fumbling with the controls to shut off the video.

"Now what?" I asked.

"Now we get the hell out of here and wait for help to arrive." He took the phone. "Move. Let's go." He pointed to the back of the shop. "Stay away from the light. Head for the trees."

I was shaking my head before he finished speaking. "There's a stream between us and the trees. There's no way to get over it anywhere near here, and it's too deep to wade. There's about twelve acres of land here. Most of the north side is trees. I don't think they've clear-cut that yet, so if we can get there, we can hide."

"Are you sure?"

"I worked on this land for thirty years. I'm sure. Roy's landscape office and the nursery store were over by the stream. Every spring we had to keep an eye on the stream in case it flooded." I thought frantically. "Come on. This way." I headed for what used to be the west end of the building. If my drugged recollections were correct, I was brought in from the south side on the road that had led to the shop. If we could get around to the back side of the store, we might be able to get to the trees on the north side. Then we could hunker down there and wait for the cavalry to arrive.

Royal tapped in a number on the phone and spoke into it as we made our way out of my ruined store. "We're at the demolition site for the DeWitt Nursery," he said in a soft voice to whoever answered. "I think they're still on-site."

I picked my way through snow and darkness, feeling my way cautiously among the ruin of what used to be a patio where I displayed yard art and bird baths. Royal was moving okay but limping, and his right arm hung at his side. It was hard to tell in the spotty light, but he seemed exhausted. Shock, probably. I prayed it wasn't anything more serious than that.

I stopped when I got to the corner of the building. Straight ahead of me on the north were what appeared to be enormous monsters. Then I realized it was construction machinery—a bulldozer, one of those claw-things like in the kid's arcade, and two big things I thought of as 'squishers'. They had tank-like tread and seemed to crouch, lurking and waiting to crush anything in their path.

I turned back to Royal. He was still on the phone, leaning against the wall of the building. "Okay," he said softly. "Yeah. We need to hide. We're both hurt, and I'm unarmed." He listened some more. "Okay." He lowered the phone and jammed it into his back pocket. "They're on the way. Slow down. Let me check ahead."

I held up my hand and peeked around the remnants of the fence that delineated the patio from the parking area. I glimpsed movement on my right, coming out of the darkness from the area where we arrived. I turned, but Royal was faster. He paused, stooped, picked up a board, and met the man running toward us head-on, swinging the board like a baseball bat. The man went down but didn't stay down.

Royal kicked him, lifting the board for another blow. The man raised a gun. I stood there, paralyzed like an idiot. Royal dodged. They struggled, grunting and heaving in the snow. I flailed around for a weapon of some kind, another board or a crowbar or something.

Royal suddenly was standing, the gun in his hand. The man started to get to his feet. Royal fired point-blank into the man's face. The sound was muffled, but I could smell it. I think I felt it when the man's face exploded.

"Oh, God," I rasped, my throat suddenly so dry I choked.

Royal looked over his shoulder, and our eyes met. I saw apprehension, determination, and regret. Not regret for killing the man but regret that I saw him do it. I remembered what Joe the actor said: *It's not every woman who can handle having an FBI agent as a boyfriend*. Now that I saw him for what he was, would it matter?

The thoughts raced through my mind in the time it took to blink. Did it matter that he could kill a man like that?

Hell, no. Not today, it didn't. I ran to his side. His mouth twisted in that half-smile of his, then he slowly dropped to his knees.

"Are you okay?" I leaned over him.

"My arm is screwed up. The recoil got me. I think it's dislocated. I'm tired, too." He peered up at me. "Shock."

I nodded. "Let's find a place to hide." I put an arm around him and got him on his feet. We staggered ahead to one of the squishers, but I could tell he wasn't going to be able to go far. Damn it. I wanted to be a superhero. Wonder Woman or Lara Croft. But I was just me. What could I do? I didn't have magic bracelets or martial arts training. What could I do?

I sucked in a deep breath. I could try to keep him alive. That was the best I could do. We struggled through the snow, reaching the shelter of the machine. I ducked between the huge treads, pulling Royal in after me. It was relatively snow-free, and the bulk of the treads blocked the wind. Royal sank to the ground, obviously exhausted.

I sat down next to him and wrapped my arms around his body, trying to give him some warmth and block him from the snow falling into the declivity. "Hang on," I spoke into his ear. "It won't be long. Somebody will get here."

He rested his head against my shoulder. "Thanks for that vote of confidence back there." His breath was warm against my neck.

"What?"

"You think you could love me?"

I pulled away to peer down at him. His face was haggard with pain, but I saw warmth and humor in his eyes. "Maybe."

"Good." He closed his eyes, his shoulders sagging. "I think I could, too."

I rested on his outstretched legs, trying to cover as much of him as I could with my body. We sat like that for a second then Royal whispered, "We need to move. We're trapped in here. Come on." He held out his hand. "Take this. I can't use my arm. I need my other arm to maneuver."

He was holding out the gun. "I can't take that. I don't know how to shoot."

"It's simple. Aim, point, and squeeze. There's no safety. All you have to do is point and shoot."

"I thought all guns had safety switches." I knew next to nothing about guns, but I had seen that in innumerable cop shows on TV.

"It has a safety, but you don't have to flip a switch. There's a safety bar on the trigger that stops you from accidentally discharging it. Just take it, aim, and squeeze. Don't be afraid of it. You probably won't hit anything, but you'll slow somebody down."

I started to answer then I heard voices. I moved away from Royal to stand, but he pulled me back down, putting his fingers to his lips. He inched upward, peeking out of our hiding place. "They're coming back," he breathed.

I hunkered down, praying the darkness would hide my red top. Royal put his good arm around me, pulling me close. We pressed back into the shadows, listening to the crunch of feet coming toward us through snow-covered leaves.

"He's fucking crazy," one voice said. "Who cares if the bitch got away? It's time we got away."

"I don't know," another voice said. This was Santa Claus man. I recognized his faintly Southern accent. "He usually knows what he's doing. We got away with all the other ones. It's like he's losing his mind on this one."

"Okay. Let's just tell him we did a sweep and we can't find 'em. I don't know about you, but I don't plan to die for him. Hell, he's dead on his feet already." The voice was getting quieter with each word. They were walking away.

"I'm not that dead." I recognized that voice. It was the wavering, icy voice of Hunter Mann. The voice came from our left, just outside the tread where we crouched. I looked at Royal, my heart pounding so loud I was sure someone would hear me. He shook his head, his arm tight around me.

"Hey, we checked everywhere. Can't see anything in this snow with all this crap lying around. They'll die of the cold soon anyway."

"You're right. No one can see anything in this snow."

The gunshot was so loud I jumped against Royal's arm, my immediate instinct to run as fast as I could. He pulled me down hard. I hit the metal of the tread with my head, making the world spin for a second.

"Get the car." This was Mann again.

"Sure, yeah. I'm on it. Just wait here. I'll bring it here." That was Santa Claus man, his voice frantic and pleading.

"Bring it to the side. I'll meet you there. I want to check one last time."

"Are you sure? You're so sick, can you—?"

"I've told you before. I don't care if I die today. I want to see her body. If I can only see her body, I'll happily die. Get the car."

"Right. Yeah."

Someone ran past, panting with deep gasping breaths while he labored through the snow. Mann was still out there. But how could he be? He had been barely moving when I saw him earlier. How could he be out here in a snowstorm?

"You're out here, Snow. I know you are." His shout filled our small space.

I held my breath, praying that he wouldn't come nearer. If he bent over he'd see us, hiding between the treads of this monster machine. We'd be sitting ducks. We'd have no chance.

Royal slowly released me, gently moving me to one side. I knew what he was going to do. He was going to try to jump out and distract Mann. I shook my head frantically. *No*, I mouthed. *Don't*.

Royal tried to get his legs under him, inching forward cautiously. He set the gun down on the ground because he couldn't use his right arm. All he had was his left arm to support himself. I heard the steps outside, not far from us. Just a few feet away.

I focused on the darkness of the entry to our small hideaway. A shadow fell, caused by the overhead light of the security lamp.

Royal gathered himself in a crouch, like an off-balance sprinter getting ready to burst out of the gate.

I picked up the gun and barreled past Royal.

Mann was standing on my left, leaning on a cane. He held a gun, too. It swung up when I came floundering out into the snow. The gun wasn't pointed at me. Mann was pointing it at Royal while he staggered to his feet, lurching for Mann.

I forgot about the gun I held. All I could think about was pushing the gun that Mann held away from Royal. I lunged, knocking into Mann. He went flying backward, landing like some skeletal snow angel.

Sirens wailed nearby, somewhere in front of my old store. Mann propped himself up on his elbows, the gun still in his hand. Now it was aimed at me.

I stood over Mann. I thought of Brainy and Bitchy. Sporty. The other women who died. I heard Royal's voice in my head. *It's hard to kill someone.*

"No, it isn't," I said.

I pulled the trigger.

Chapter 14

Royal was right. It actually is hard to kill somebody.

When I pulled the trigger, the gun bucked in my hand. I was aiming for Mann's chest, but I hit his shoulder instead. I was so surprised by the noise and the recoil that I fired again. I missed him completely. I guess I was disoriented because I dropped the gun and ran to Royal, cowering behind him.

Mann lay at our feet, unconscious. "It's okay." Royal sagged against me. "It's over."

My knees trembled, and I sank down, landing on my butt in the snow and taking Royal with me. We sat there, our arms around each other.

The sound of the shots told the police where we were. The hospital staff had alerted the police to a stolen ambulance. Vaughan figured out what I was saying, so they got to us in record time. Well, that and commandeering a snowplow to keep the roads clear for them meant they had no troubles due to the snowstorm.

Royal and I were whisked to the hospital. I had a minor case of frostbite and lots of bruises. Royal had all kinds of contusions and broken ribs and other stuff that, had I known about it, I wouldn't have dragged him around the construction site. As he said, it was probably good I didn't know because now we were alive. He had a point.

I had to make a statement about the shooting. Essentially I told them that I did what Royal told me to do. I aimed the gun and pulled the trigger. I wasn't really trying to kill Mann. Maybe. I'm still not sure about that.

"I aimed for the chest because it seemed hard to miss," I told the cold-faced detective who questioned me.

He shot me a disbelieving look. "And yet you did."

"How about that. I've never handled a gun before in my life. I'm glad I didn't shoot myself in the foot."

He seemed appeased by my answer, and they didn't bug me much after that.

Mann was taken into custody, but he never came to trial. He died before they could even convene the grand jury. The bastard never had to answer for his crimes. Or maybe he's answering for them now. I can hope.

My father was released from the hospital. Aurora and I came up with a plan for home health care. Roy spends two days and nights each week at my place, one day at a senior center, and the rest of the time he's at home with at-home nursing as needed. That gives Aurora a break from full-time care, and it gives me a chance to spend time with him.

She and I have worked out a truce of sorts, at least as far as Roy is concerned. I encouraged her to start taking classes while Roy is still around to give her advice. I think he enjoys helping her with her landscaping assignments, and she's benefiting from his years of experience. A win-win all around.

I came to peace with the loss of my business. I think seeing it as a murder zone helped a lot to make me less nostalgic about the place. I slowly began to enjoy being retired. It helps that Royal has become a regular player in my life. But before that happened, he and I had a little heart-to-heart talk to clear up any questions about our relationship.

It happened one day when I caught him inspecting my cookware. This was about two months after he got out of the hospital. "You really need to get some better pans," he said.

"You know, we're not really compatible." I crossed my arms, watching him disdain my choice of skillets.

"Why not?"

"We have nothing in common. For cryin' out loud, think about it. We're only together because we were both scared silly by a madman. Once that excitement wears off, you'll see. We just don't suit each other."

He tilted his head and regarded me. "Fast food or restaurant?"

"Huh?"

"You heard me. Fast food or restaurant?"

"Restaurant," I said quickly when he took a step toward me. "Lord knows where the food came from at some of those fast-food places."

"Jeans or polyester?"

I made a rude noise. "Jeans."

"Chick flicks or action movies?" He moved closer. I backed up, only to find the counter behind me.

"Action. Give me an unbelievable plot any day."

"Some chick flicks are pretty unbelievable." One corner of his mouth quirked up in a half-smile. "Winter or summer?" Now he was just a foot or so away from me.

"Winter. Definitely winter. I can always get warm, but it's hard to cool off."

"Good to know," he said in a low voice. I shivered at the sound.

"So you see—we're not compatible."

"I'd say we're really compatible. Except for a few areas."

I eyed him suspiciously. "Does that mean all the stuff on your profile is a fraud?"

The tips of his ears got red. "I wouldn't say a fraud. Maybe just not quite what I would have said. Vaughn filled it out for me. He told me that he knew what would attract you."

"Does that mean you don't like country music? You don't like rock and roll?"

Royal shook his head. "Can't stand it."

"Wait a minute." I nestled in closer to him, pressing my hips against his. "What about the Boot-Scootin' Boogie?"

His lips curved up in a faint smile. "Well, maybe."

"And it seems to me you told me that you like it, you love it, and you want some more of it." I moved even closer, my lips just inches from his.

"If you put it that way…I guess I don't mind some country and western music."

"Just some?"

"Hmm."

Yeah, teaching him the finer points of line dancing is keeping me pretty darn busy. And he's teaching me about acting and singing and stage craft. I've worked on some sets for a play he's rehearsing. The other day I heard him practicing "Some Enchanted Evening" in the shower, and my heart just about stopped.

That was some enchanted evening for us. If you know what I mean.

Four months after that snowstorm, Royal, Vaughan, Finn, and I went to Florida. Royal waited for us outside Nimble's hospital room. Nimble lay on the bed, hooked up to monitors, with things stuck into his arms and other parts of the body I didn't want to think about.

We had talked to his kids just an hour or so earlier. They came to a painful decision, and it wouldn't be long now. We all approached the bed. A tall Black man stood on the opposite side, staring down at the shell of the man who had once been a dear friend. The stranger nodded to us when we neared.

"I'm an old college friend." I placed my hand on Nimble's forearm where it rested outside the bed clothes. "We all went to school together."

Vaughan went to the head of the bed and smiled down at our old friend. Finn stood between us, his gaze on Brian's face. Brian's eyes were closed, and his cheeks were sunken. He was no longer the handsome, macho baseball player. I could only see a shadow of that man in the frail patient lying on the bed.

"He mentioned you. You must be Snow White." I looked up in surprise. The man smiled. He was very muscular, with short hair, dark skin, and startling white teeth. "Nimble and I were teammates. I played left field."

"Nimble," I murmured. "It was such an apt name."

"He told us all about you guys. Snow White and the Seven Jocks." The man's gaze shifted to all of us, one after the other, with a puzzled frown. "Wasn't there something in the newspaper a while back about you? Wasn't there some trouble?"

"Yeah, but it's all done now." I leaned over Brian

and kissed his cheek. "It's over," I said, my lips near his ear. He smelled of soap and antiseptic, his skin cool. "They caught the guy, and he's dead. It won't bring anyone back, but at least it's done now. Say hello to Sporty for me. Tell her I found my guy. Tell her I'm happy." I straightened and touched Brian's still-thick dark hair. "I just wanted to see him one last time."

Vaughan leaned over and brushed his lips against Brian's forehead. "We'll miss you, Nimble."

Finn squeezed Brian's forearm. "You're going to the Field of Dreams now. Have fun, old friend."

"I'll be sorry to lose him, but I know he wouldn't want to be here like this." The man smiled down at Brian, his eyes bright with tears. "The doctor said he could last for years, but I don't think he'd want that. Better to be gone."

"Yes," I said. I remembered the handsome, energetic young man who used to excel at sports. Then I remembered the twisted, agonized man who had caused all this grief. Mann had lasted for years, taking his anger and pain and morphing it into an excuse for murder and revenge. "Better to be gone." I touched Brian's hand one last time then turned to go.

"Thank you for coming," the man said. "It's hard for people to face, I know."

I gazed at Nimble. We were so young then. We had no idea that the things we did would have such consequences. I knew that we did nothing wrong all those years ago. Yet Hunter Mann blamed us for his life and how it turned out. It was important to me that Nimble knew it was over. We could rest.

We left the room. Royal was leaning against the opposite wall. When I came out, he straightened, and I went into his arms. "Are you okay?" he asked, his chin resting on my head.

I nodded. "All fine." We walked out of the hospital together, me with my arm around my Prince Charming.